Three Split Seconds
Melissa Smith

Copyright © 2024 by Melissa Smith

All rights reserved.

No portion of this book may be reproduced in any form without written permission from the publisher or author, except as permitted by U.S. copyright law.

MORE BY MELISSA

WHAT I DIDN'T DO
A Bar Harbor Psychological Thriller

Melissa also writes erotic romance under the pen name Mel S.

DEMON ESHA TRILOGY
Demon Esha
Becoming Esha
Desiring Esha
EMBER

Contents

1. ONE — 1
2. TWO — 21
3. THREE — 46
4. FOUR — 66
5. FIVE — 85
6. SIX — 98
7. SEVEN — 110
8. EIGHT — 128
9. NINE — 142
10. TEN — 160
11. ELEVEN — 174
12. TWELVE — 191

ONE

The martini glass in front of me tipped forward, falling to the shiny wooden bar top. It shattered into shards of glass. All the other patrons looked my way while the bartender hurried over with his rag.

"I'm...I'm sorry," I babbled.

"Can I get you some water, miss?" he suggested, not even trying to hide his irritation.

"No," I said. "I should go."

He placed my bill on the bar, barely missing the spilled vodka. I reached for it, but before I could touch it, a hand to the right of mine snatched it away.

"I'll get it." A middle-aged man smiled at me.

"What? No." I was astonished. We hadn't even talked, and this stranger wanted to pay?

"I insist," he replied. He handed the skinny paper to the woman sitting next to him. She took it and passed it back to the bartender along with a credit card.

"Thank you," I stuttered. "Thank you very much..."

"Vince," he said. "And this is my wife, Nadia."

The woman leaned over and smiled at me. I smiled back suspiciously, unsure of what was happening.

"I didn't mean to startle you," Vince apologized. "It looked like you were having a bad day, so I thought..."

"Thank you," I interrupted him. "Your kindness is lovely."

"Do you want to stay? We can get a table?" he offered.

"No, no, thank you. I should go." I stood up.

"Do you need a ride somewhere?" Vince was overly helpful.

I slowly backed away and bumped directly into a server with a tray full of fish and chip specials. The server, the tray, and I all clattered to the ground. Seagulls soared overhead, impatiently waiting to clean up the mess. I didn't say anything as I crawled to my feet and all but ran down the pier. I stopped just out of sight of the makeshift restaurant. I sat down on a wooden bench overlooking the water. This inlet was home to the residents of Camden, Maine, a place so beautiful it could be a calendar photo even on the rainiest of days. The little cove housed countless sailboats as well as gorgeous yachts and simple fishing vessels. The Maine coastline was rugged, demanding attention and reverence. The wind whipping in my face was no different.

It was fall here in Camden. These seasonal pop-up culinary boutiques would all be closed after Columbus Day next week, if they weren't already. Honestly, I hadn't expected this spot to be open today, what with the storm and all. Hurricanes up this far were rarely a cause for concern. Yes, you'd need an umbrella, which I didn't have, but it wasn't like down south where they had to board up windows and sandbag streets.

The sky far out over the horizon looked angry, matching my twenty-seven-year-old soul. The water lapped against the rocking boats tied up in the harbor. I felt like one of those tiny ships, fighting against the tie that held me tight. I shivered in the early October drizzle before realizing I'd left my jacket at the bar. I closed my eyes, feeling utterly defeated. I held my face up to the raindrops that were starting to come faster, wishing the water would wipe away my worries.

"Hey there." I heard Vince's voice behind me. "You forgot your jacket." He walked around to the front of the bench and held my favorite faux leather jacket out to me.

"Oh, thank you!" I happily took it from him.

"Are you sure you're okay?" he asked. His voice was calm and smooth, soothing even.

"I'm sure I'm not okay." I laughed sarcastically. "But I do appreciate the concern."

"I put our cell numbers in the pocket." Vince pointed casually to the jacket now draped over my shoulders. "If you need anything, please don't hesitate to call." With that, he turned and walked away.

I watched him saunter back toward the bar and I wondered: What makes some people so nice and other people such assholes? Is it luck? Fate? Learned behavior? I have always been interested in the psychology of human behavior. It was such a mystery at times. I knew all about conditioning and nature vs. nurture, but my time in the real world had proven to me that it was 100% a crap shoot. People only cared if they wanted something. It was quite simple.

Perhaps that was my freshly printed divorce papers talking. Or maybe it was all the shredded photos of his affairs that were now nestled in the bottom of my trash can at home. I'd blown all my extra money on that damn private investigator only to be shown proof of what I already knew to be true. Now I was even poorer than before with no relief in sight. I had no place to live, no one to love, and no hope for a brighter future. Seven years of my life had been a complete waste of time, not to mention energy. There should be a law against marrying too young. The human brain isn't even finished developing yet in your early twenties. You shouldn't be able to make life-altering decisions so young. Especially ones where you'll end up with shit credit and emotional scars that will accompany you for the rest of your life.

I knew that thought process was foolish. We had to make choices and decisions to grow. I knew I'd move on. I'd rally and bounce back, eventually. But this minute, it felt right, fitting even, to sit here slumped over in the chilling rains of a hurricane.

What should I do now? I served him with divorce papers last night. I went to their hotel room, proclaiming to be room service, and promptly handed him the sealed folder containing directions for separating the life we'd built. To serve your husband divorce papers while he is covered only in a bath towel and hanging on the arm of his mistress is quite a feat. I'd dolled myself up for the occasion, but the emptiness I'd felt after deflated any sense of ego my new shoes had previously provided.

"Thanks, doll," he replied and closed the door in my face. I knew he wouldn't fight for me. We'd been over long before my need for proof, however, I wasn't prepared for the hope of explanation that had crept up into my throat. He didn't explain anything. He looked relieved. Like maybe I'd saved him some paperwork. I drove home and packed anything I wanted, which wasn't much. Clothes mostly. Then I checked into a hotel in the next town: Camden.

Now, as I sat and watched the storm pass by the gray harbor, something caught my eye. A swarm of birds and fish were picking at something floating in the water. As whatever it was floated inland, I began to recognize the shape of a body. The frame appeared to be approximately six feet long. It bobbed and swayed with the angry ocean waters, bumping into boats and docks as it went.

Suddenly I heard a voice cry out: "A body! There's a body!"

Then there was the trampling of feet on the pier as a crowd formed near the floating corpse. I watched from my bench, soaked from the rain that was now coming in sheets. It was as if the storm had changed its mind and decided to drift inland after all, accompanying the dead body perhaps. As I sat there, a feeling of dread crept up my spine. I knew whose body it was, and what's more, I knew I had no choice but to call the number in my pocket.

I didn't call Vince. My trust in men had reached an all-time low. I stared at his number, written neatly next to his wife's, and then I crumpled up the paper and tossed it into a puddle. I unzipped my secret pocket and pulled out my private investigator's card. I studied it, twirling it around in my fingers as I tried to decide whether or not I should make a deal with the devil himself. I'd known Tanner Wilden since we were children, way before he became Tanner Wilden, PI. He was always a mean, nosey boy. Always butting into everyone else's business. Always looking for dirt and drama. I hadn't been surprised at all when I'd heard he'd become a PI. He was very well suited for it.

My fingers hovered over the call button on my phone. I knew he could protect me and if I was right, if the body being eaten by minnows was my husband's, I'd need protection. I'd need more than protection. I'd need a new start even more than I already did. Tanner could give me a new start, and he'd jump at the chance. He'd expressed interest in me several times during our weeks of working together. I'd always giggled away his advances, for the most part.

Just then, a blonde woman ran down the ramp to the pier, screaming as she went.

"Michael! Michael!" she screeched.

It's funny how your body reacts to trauma. How your instincts kick in and fight-or-flight takes over naturally. I knew it was Michael before she showed up; before she flailed herself over my husband's half-eaten face. I knew it was him, and I knew she killed him. I had heard them yelling as I walked away from their hotel room. She'd had no idea he was married. Classic, I'd thought as I walked away. Now here she was, grieving over our lying man, her tears mixing with the salt and blood draining from his flesh. I pressed the call button and closed my eyes, knowing full well I was jumping from the frying pan into the fire.

"You've got Tanner," said the voice on the other end of the line.

"It's me." I cleared my throat.

"Is it time?" he asked after a brief pause.

"Yes," I admitted with a shrug.

"I'll be right there." The phone clicked.

Of course he knew where I was. No doubt he'd put a tracker on my car ages ago. Tanner was the type of man who was accustomed to getting what he wanted. Perhaps I should have called Vince and Nadia, but they seemed far too nice and innocent to be dragged into my drama.

I walked up the hill to the parking lot. The wind and rain beat angrily against my body as I walked. I was almost to my car when another car pulled up beside me and the passenger window rolled down. I leaned over expecting to see Tanner, but instead, Nadia smiled back at me.

"Hey, girl! I was just coming to check on you. Are you good?" She smiled as though her face were used to the position, as if it would pain her to not smile. I didn't say a word, just stared at her with a blank expression on my face. "Do you want to get in? It's really coming down now!" I heard the passenger door unlock.

Should I? I reasoned with myself. Nadia seemed nice. She had a pale complexion and glistening jet-black hair. Upon first glance, you'd think she'd be caked to the gills with makeup, but she wasn't. Suddenly I heard Tanner's truck jostling down the old side street, and I threw caution to the wind and quickly climbed into Nadia's car. I ducked down in the seat.

"I was going to go with him. The guy in the truck," I explained, keeping myself out of sight. "I'd rather go with you."

"You got it." Nadia grinned.

We made our way back out to US Route 1. My phone rang shortly thereafter. I stared at it. I knew it was Tanner. The unknown number didn't fool me.

"Are you going to answer that?" Nadia asked.

"No." I paused. "You know, this is probably a bad idea. You should let me out. I don't want to drag you into my mess." I sighed heavily.

"It's fine," Nadia assured me. "You look like someone who could use a friend. That's all."

"A friend," I repeated. "Boy, it's been a while since I've had a friend."

"Then it's settled!" She grinned even bigger than before and turned up the radio. Pop music brought me back to my high school days.

"Let me just toss this..." I held my phone up to the window.

"Wait." Nadia stopped me. "We can burn it or something. Burning is always better. Is it bugged?"

"I don't think so. My car, though, that's probably bugged."

"Well, it's a good thing you're with me then!" She laughed. With that, we cranked up the radio, all my worries temporarily vanishing away as we sang along with our high school crushes.

"My name is Macie," I said between songs. "And thank you."

"Vince and I are staying here in town. We're at a big castle-looking place up here on the right," Nadia explained.

"The Norumbega, that place is beautiful," I approved.

"We can pick up Vince and grab a drink somewhere if you'd like?"

"Is there any chance we could stay in?" I asked, hoping I didn't sound creepy. "I just...well, I've landed myself in quite a predicament."

"Of course!" Nadia beamed. "We have a suite with a sitting room. We'll pop a bottle of champagne and chat. Or if you'd rather be left alone, we can do that too."

"I'd rather not be alone," I whispered, gazing out the window at all the perfectly manicured hedges and lawns.

The castle wasn't far from Sea Street. In no time, Nadia had made me feel as comfortable as possible in their suite. The place was just as beautiful inside as it was out. Brick walls lined the exterior sides, while crisp freshly painted white walls brightened up the interior. The white was a sharp contrast to the maroon of the bricks and dark woodwork. We gathered in their adjacent sitting room, munching on a platter of homemade macaroons.

Half a bottle in, I started to loosen up. I'd learned Vince and Nadia were here from Laconia, New Hampshire. They were on vacation, scouting oceanside properties for retirement. Nadia didn't appear to be much older than me, but Vince was pushing fifty and liked to be informed and prepared. Upon initial assessment, I guessed he was a Capricorn, but when I heard him talk about the ocean and the beauty he found in the depths of the waves, I instead pegged him as a water sign. Scorpio, probably.

As we finished the first bottle of champagne, I finally spilled the beans. I set my glass on the coffee table in front of the Renaissance-style couch and took a long deep breath.

"You guys seem like really great people," I started. "I either need to get out of here or be honest."

"Oh Macie, you're very sweet." Nadia twirled her hair with one slender finger. "Honesty is always preferred, but there is no pressure."

"I would like to talk to someone," I paused. "But I don't want to put you guys in an uncomfortable spot."

They didn't seem uncomfortable in the least. In fact, I was picking up on some very distracting sexual vibes from Nadia and I wanted badly to reciprocate but I felt I needed to confide in them first.

"I know you don't know me, and I don't know you, but I am in a predicament." One more deep breath and I continued. "I served my husband with divorce papers last night and this afternoon his body floated into the cove." I picked my glass back up and swallowed what champagne I had left.

"Oh, honey!" Nadia slid closer to me on the couch and put her arm around my shoulder.

Vince stood up and went to the minibar for another bottle of bubbly.

"I know we're not celebrating," he said. "But I feel like we need more alcohol."

"I agree." I felt tears spring to my eyes. They weren't mad or disappointed or scared. They were supportive. I held my glass up to Vince and he refilled it.

"We're very sorry for your loss." Vince topped off all three glasses and sat back down in his chair.

"So, obviously you didn't do it, or I can't imagine you'd be here talking about it."

"Correct." I nodded. "Truthfully, it's not much of a loss. We weren't close."

"Maybe don't word things quite like that, honey." Nadia coached me from her seat on the edge of the couch. "It's fine with us, but if you talk to anyone else…"

"Nadia, you're not at work right now," Vince scolded her.

"I know, but she should know," Nadia chirped back at him.

"It's okay, she's right." I chuckled at them. "I shouldn't incriminate myself."

"Are you a lawyer?" Nadia asked, intrigued.

"No, but I've watched an awful lot of Matlock with my Gram." I smiled. "Anyway, no, I didn't do it, but I'm pretty sure I know who did, and she's going to set me up for the fall. I'm sure of it."

"Who?" Vince asked with one eyebrow raised.

"His mistress." I rolled my eyes. The word sounded foreign rolling off my tongue. Did people even use that reference anymore? Was that just a television term? It felt gross coming out of my mouth.

I sat there and told these friendly strangers the pathetic story of my marriage. How Michael and I met and fell in love in college. How he was a basketball star and how I pined after him so unapologetically. We were introduced at a party, and he thought I looked pretty hanging on his arm. I was an accessory to his stardom, and it was hard not to like the glamor and glitz of it all. At first, it was a rush for me, a sense of accomplishment even. We were married our senior year of college. After graduation, when we got out in the real world, Michael bored with me fairly quickly. He needed fame and applause. It fueled him. I was a cute wife to come home to, but nothing more.

I knew he was sleeping with other people almost instantly. It wasn't the late meetings or the cryptic text messages that gave it away. It was his mood. He became happier almost overnight. It couldn't have been more obvious. I played dumb. I liked my life, for the most part. Michael was a good provider, and he always took care of my needs when time allowed. Over the months and years that followed, 'when time allowed' became my least favorite phrase, yet I never strayed. I never went elsewhere for my needs or satisfaction. Until I did. That's when I decided I wanted a divorce.

I hired Tanner Wilden, PI to investigate and get proof for me. I wanted proof before I filed for divorce. Finally, proof in hand, I'd filled out the divorce papers and given Michael his copy, but I hadn't filed anything. We still had to sign them. My copy was sitting on the front seat of my Subaru. Surely the cops would find it when they found my car. At this point, I had no idea if I was a wanted person yet or not.

"So, why do you think she did it?" Vince asked.

"She was pretty mad when I left them at the hotel. I could hear her screaming at him from the parking lot. She was letting on like she didn't know he was married," I explained.

"Oh." Vince sat back in his chair, rubbing his salt and pepper goatee like he was deep in thought.

"Fuck," Nadia cursed softly. It surprised me to hear such a vulgar word come from her pretty plump lips.

"So, you need an alibi." Vince clapped his hands together firmly and stood up. He paced the room before turning to face Nadia and me. "I know!" He clicked his fingers and pointed them at me. "You were with us. Here."

"That's perfect!" Nadia approved wholeheartedly.

"Are you...are you sure?" I stammered.

"Hell yeah!" Nadia bounced around excitedly on the couch. "In fact, here..." She squirmed around until she flicked her thong off her ankle. She caught it in mid-air and handed it to me. "Put this on! That way, you'll have proof you were here, with us!"

I blushed. They'd thought of everything. "I can't do that," I objected. "I'm divorcing him on grounds of infidelity. I can't do the same thing to him."

"Honey, he's dead." She laid her hand on my thigh. "You're a widow, not a divorcee."

"Damn," I whispered and sat back.

Everyone was quiet. The power flickered and then went out. I carefully set my glass on the coffee table and stood up.

"You're sure?" I asked in the darkness.

"Of course!" Nadia promised.

"Alright." I blew out a deep breath and unzipped my jeans. I let them fall to the floor at my feet and I wriggled out of them. I slipped my thumbs into the waistband of my white lace thong and pushed it down my legs. Then I stepped into Nadia's thong and slid it up into place around my hips. I put my jeans back on and settled down on the couch, just as the castle generator kicked on and light illuminated the room once again.

TWO

My name is Macie Alexandra Black. I was born and raised in Boston. Most people leave New England after they finish high school. Not me. I went North, to Vacationland, to the University of Maine Orono. I went for their veterinary program, but instead of a degree in Agriculture and Veterinary Services, I got distracted and married. Now here I was, lying on the far edge of a plush king-size bed wondering if the two people lying next to me would snore all night. I snore. I know I do. Michael used to bitch about it.

Tonight, my thoughts were far from sleep. I held my breath, waiting for someone to knock on the door. No doubt they'd identified Michael's remains by now. Surely, they were trying to reach me. Did it make me look guilty that I was hiding here? It certainly didn't make me look innocent. I wasn't sure what to do. Run or stay? Part of me longed to run, to hide, to become someone else. To not be Michael's widow. Part of me wanted to stay and find justice, to face his murderer and feel vindication, but that part of me was very, very, very small. I had an alibi. I had a clear conscience. I should stay. Only chaos would follow me if I ran.

I didn't burn my phone. That would have looked very suspicious. I shut it off and let Vince look it over for bugs. It appeared to be clean. I kept it shut off anyway. I liked the fact that no one knew where I was. This felt like the adventure of a lifetime, probably because I was still buzzed from the excessive amount of champagne I'd drank. It was nice to sit, talk, and drink with friends. I recognized the fact that they were actually strangers, but I reveled in the authenticity that seemed to surround them.

I didn't have a lot of friends. As my world became more and more consumed with Michael and basketball, my friends faded away. I can't say as I blamed them. That's what happens in life. People change and pick sides. No one stays who they were. Or at least, that's how it seemed to go for me and my friends. Now, on the other side of the love bubble, I realized I was the one who most likely pulled away from them. I had Michael. I had no room for girlfriends. Sad but true, and now I was reaping the subtle benefits of having no one to say the dreaded phrase: I told you so.

As I lay in bed, I thought about the moment when my husband's mistress first saw his body bobbing in the water of the cove. She had done a stellar job pretending to be upset. She'd screamed, screeched even, one of those blood-curdling screams that draws attention from anyone within hearing distance. She'd fallen to her knees on the pier. It took two big men to hold her back from Michael's body. She'd been beyond distraught. Suddenly the thought occurred to me: What if she didn't do it? She didn't seem like the actress type. Lord knows what she'd told the authorities about me by now. I could only imagine. I'd been so icy with Michael when I served him the divorce papers. I'd believe I killed him...

Just then I realized I had no choice. I had to go. I couldn't stay here. If I thought I did it, everyone else would think that too. I quietly got out of bed and dressed. I gathered my shoes and bag and headed for the door. The rain was pounding down outside. I could hear it pelting against the windows. I stopped at the door and walked back to the end table where I quickly wrote a note to Vince and Nadia.

'I'm sorry. I can't stay. Thank you both for everything. You're angels.'

I wanted to sign my name or M, but I didn't. I knew I had to be on high alert from here on out. I put the pen down next to the notebook with the castle logo on it. Then I thought better of it, picked the pen back up, and continued writing.

'P.S. - I borrowed your car. You can find it at...'

Suddenly the light clicked on, and Vince stood beside me, naked. I was caught red-handed, and crimson quickly claimed every inch of my skin as I stared at all of him. He bent down and picked up the notepad. I watched his expression as he read what I'd written.

"An honest thief," he smirked and tossed the pad back on the table.

"I'm sorry!" I whispered, not wanting to wake Nadia. "I can't stay here and it's raining outside. I'm not a thief. I was just borrowing…"

"By all means." He held the keys out to me, dangling them between my eyes. I watched them glint back and forth in the lamplight. It was then I realized he was stroking himself. He stepped closer to me and whispered in my ear. "Or you can stay. I can protect you."

"With that?" I snickered, motioning to his penis while trying not to look at it.

"Precisely," he groaned.

"I'll walk," I said, annoyed, and turned to leave.

"Wait." He all but tripped over the end table as he tried to stop me. "I'm sorry! Look, I can't help it, two gorgeous women in bed with me."

"This is serious," I hissed softly, my demeanor changing to fragile without my consent.

"I know." He rubbed my shoulders. "You can take the car. What's your plan? You're going to hop on a bus and head where?"

"I'm not sure yet," I admitted.

"This is where people fuck up," Vince schooled me. "They rush and jump into things with no plan. You need to think this through. Let me help you."

"Alright," I nodded. "What do you suggest?"

"Let me find my shorts and we'll chat, okay?" He gauged my reaction to see if I would bolt before he walked to the other side of the bed in search of clothing. He came back with boxers on and made us each a cup of coffee with the fanciest Keurig I'd ever seen. We sat down on the couch in the sitting room. I'd pulled all the curtains closed when it started to get dark out. I hated feeling paranoid. It ate at me from the inside out, nauseating yet invigorating at the same time.

"What do you want? What's your end goal?" Vince asked.

"I don't want this hanging over me. I don't want to go to jail." I answered.

"But what *do* you want?" he reiterated.

"I want to be cleared of any guilt," I said without hesitation.

"Then you can't run," Vince proclaimed. "You can't hide."

I didn't respond. I knew he was right. I hated this nervous feeling. If I ran, I'd feel this way for the rest of my life. Michael would control me from the grave. That was the last thing I wanted.

"I get in my head too much," I chuckled softly. "I know I can't run. I don't want to run. I'm just...I'm just scared."

"I'm sure you are!" Vince sympathized. "Everything you do from this point on will directly determine who you are when you come out on the other side of this. And you will come out on the other side. This won't last forever."

"I feel so alone." I fought back tears. Michael had been my only person for so long. He hadn't been a great person, but he'd been mine, even if not solely mine.

"You are not alone," Nadia spoke from the doorway. She looked gorgeous in her long black negligee. She joined us on the couch, snuggling into her husband's lap as we tried to form a plan.

***

Later that morning, the rain began to subside. The three of us decided it would be a good idea to venture out and see what was going on in the harbor. I wanted to peek at the restaurant parking lot to see if my car was still there. Sure enough, it was, but there was also a cop car sitting across from it.

"They're probably waiting for you to return," Vince interjected.

"Will you take me to the police station, please?" I asked from my ducked-down position in the back of their car. "I might as well get out in front of this thing."

"You sure?" Nadia looked at me in the mirror.

"Yes, I'm sure," I sighed.

"Just tell them you were with us," Nadia reminded me as if I'd forgotten. I knew I couldn't say that. I was the world's worst liar and more to the point, I'd met them at the bar. The bartender would verify, if asked, that I hadn't known them until then. I smiled at Nadia but remained silent. As we drove to the police station, I could picture everyone's faces when I walked in. They'd be beside themselves in a flurry of activity. This type of thing didn't happen here often. A murder, a body washed into the sailboats, a wife filing for divorce, and a mistress? It was the stuff of tabloids to be sure!

"You don't need to stay. I have a feeling I'll be awhile," I said when Vince parked along the curb.

"Are you sure?" Nadia turned around in her seat to look at me this time.

"Yes." I reached out and twirled a piece of her hair in my fingers. "Thank you both for everything."

"Honey, you have our numbers. I wrote them down again and put them in your jacket pocket in case they take your phone."

"Thank you. I'll never forget you guys."

And with that, I climbed out of their car and walked into the brick building. I'd never been inside the police station. I always imagined it to be a quaint quiet place, but today it was chaotic with a predicted sense of urgency. Camden was a popular destination here in Maine. It was nestled along US Route 1, blanketed in a beautiful sense of purpose; its only real goal was to make travelers slow down and appreciate the majestic beauty it no doubt stole from the heavens. From the rugged coastal terrain to the lush green pastures of farmland, not to mention the sparkling ocean stretching out to the horizon, and the boats dancing along the shore, beckoning adventure; Camden was picture-perfect. This was the land of glorious treasure, where vacations weren't just vacations; they were memories. Surely a murder would taint the image here. Every police officer inside these walls was on high alert.

When I stepped inside, all the noise ceased. The only thing I could hear was the gurgling of the coffee pot as it brewed in the corner. No one moved, which surprised me. I figured I would get tackled to the floor upon entrance. Instead, I made my way to the front desk where I somehow managed to speak.

"I'm Macie Black," I said to the woman at the large metal desk. "Is there someone here I can speak with?"

"Regarding?" she asked gruffly.

"The body in the harbor," I said. I tried not to sound panicked but I was sure she could see how fast my heart was beating in my chest.

Unless you are born and bred in Camden, no one knows you. It's like any other small town; if you're not from here, you're considered an outsider, an implant. This is especially true of people from Massachusetts. 'Masshole' is the endearing term most often used to describe those of us from the inferior southern state. There is no way to outgrow such affection or lack thereof. The woman at the front desk picked up the telephone, dialed a few numbers, and spoke incomprehensibly into the receiver. Seconds later, a stout bald man appeared from behind a closed door.

"Mrs. Black," he said and reached out for my hand. I expected him to cuff me, but he simply shook it instead. "We've been trying to reach you. I'm so sorry for your loss."

"Thank you." I tried to gauge his sincerity. By my initial analysis, he seemed quite genuine.

"Please," he said. "Right this way."

Part of me hoped he would question my arrival like Michael and I had nothing to do with the floating dead man. Part of me wanted nothing more than for him to say it was someone else. A stranger who'd met his fate too early. Part of me wanted to believe I'd imagined the entire scenario. But I knew, as Sergeant Renvick poured me a cup of coffee, that was not the case. He led me down a hallway and into an interrogation room. I was hoping for a conference room or a lounge. Now, as I tried not to look at the mirror, I wondered if his handshake had been a setup, a way to catch me off guard, a way for me to feel more comfortable so I'd let down my defenses.

"We haven't gotten the official coroner's report back yet, but they are estimating he's been dead for about a week," Sergeant Renvick explained. "It was pretty hard to tell…"

"Wait," I interrupted him. "What did you say? A week?"

"Yes ma'am. Now do you know if..."

"A week?" I asked again like I hadn't heard him the first two times.

"Yes," Renvick nodded.

"Well, then it can't be him. I just saw him the other night."

"Which night?" he asked, leaning forward in his chair.

"Two nights ago. I served him with divorce papers two nights ago." I was astonished.

"Two nights ago?" Renvick seemed astonished as well.

"Yes, before the storm." I took a deep breath. "I went to his hotel room."

"He was at a hotel?" Sergeant Renvick pried.

"Yes," I said slowly, cursing myself for offering too many details.

"Were you two having problems?"

"He was fucking his mistress," I said pointedly. So much for candor. Sergeant Todd Renvick jotted something down in his notebook. I couldn't tell what his chicken scratch said. "If you're writing I'm angry, I'm not," I continued. "I've known about it for a long time. We didn't talk about it, but I knew. I decided I wanted a divorce, so I went there to confront him."

"Why not wait for him to come home?" he asked with one eyebrow raised.

"Because he rarely came home." I looked down as the words tumbled out of my mouth.

"How did you know where he was?"

"I hired a detective a few months back. I wanted proof," I replied.

"I see." Sergeant Renvick's rich tone made my stomach twist.

"Anyway, yes, I served him with divorce papers two nights ago," I sighed.

"How did he react?" Renvick put his pen down on the table.

"Like a smug asshole," I replied honestly. "He said 'thanks doll' and slammed the door in my face."

"How did that make you feel?" He pushed me further.

"How do you think it made me feel?" I said snarkily. When he didn't reply, I continued. "It made me feel lonely."

"What did you do next?" he asked.

"Well, I listened to her scream at him for a bit, then I went home, packed my essentials, and drove here."

"Why was she screaming at him?" He asked as he again picked up his pen.

"I don't think she knew about me." I shrugged.

"I see." He rubbed his chin. "And where is home?"

"Belfast."

"His hotel room was in Belfast?" he asked for clarification.

"Yes." I nodded again. "I didn't want to stay home so I came here. I had to get away."

"I thought you said you weren't upset," Sergeant Renvick kept digging.

"I said I wasn't angry. I didn't say I wasn't upset." I eyed him carefully.

"I see." He jotted down more notes.

"Listen, this is all for nothing if it's not even him," I reminded the bald man in pressed khakis.

"Right, yes, my notes definitely say he's been deceased for at least a week. But, like I said, that's not confirmed."

"Clearly," I said, my voice more tense than I wanted it to be.

"Ma'am, have you tried calling your husband?" He could barely ask the obnoxious question without smirking.

"No," I scoffed at him. "I know it was him. She was so bereft."

"Who?"

"His mistress."

"When?"

"When she saw him in the water. She went crazy screaming and crying his name. How do you not know this?" I was floored that he seemed so unaware, but then again, I'd done the opposite thing; I fled.

"What was she doing down here? She was in Belfast too, right?"

"Yes, she was. I'm not sure…"

"Then why would she be here? Did she follow you?" He kept writing as he spoke.

I sat there quietly. It was the first time I'd thought of that. It was a valid question. What was she doing in the harbor? Shopping, during a hurricane?

***

The next morning, I sat in the park and watched the mist rolling gently across the dew-covered grass. It was like a wave of translucent energy frolicking across the land. The sky was a brilliant blue color today, not a cloud in sight. Very few people were out and about this time of day. It was my favorite time. A time when everything went a little slower. Even the boats tied up in the harbor seemed to bounce and rock a little softer in the waves. The water was eerily still today. The last remnants of the hurricane had floated out to sea. The world looked clear, unlike my muddled mind.

As I'd sat with Sergeant Todd Renvick, Vick as he said to call him, he'd received official word that the body in question was indeed Michael's. Perhaps it was a freak of nature or the stirred-up angry waters of the hurricane, but it did appear as though he'd been dead for a week. His estimated time of death was sometime last weekend. I couldn't figure it out. I wasn't a forensic analyst, but I thought the difference between a week and two days would be fairly evident. Maybe it all depended on the kindness of the sea. Either way, Michael was gone. I was a widow and probably a suspect, but that part wasn't clear. I'd told the truth, and I gave Vick my hotel information so he could verify my check-in time. I was free to go. They apologized for the delay in identification and didn't even tell me to stay in town. I was not a concern.

While I was in the police station with Vick, they brought in Michael's mistress for questioning. Annaleese, her name was. Vick informed me after she left that she wasn't a suspect either. She was grieving more than me. She passed a polygraph test. She was too blonde and ditzy to form a lie. Damn blondes, I thought.

So the question remained. Who killed Michael? Did he slip on the edge of the water, on a wet rock perhaps? Did he drink too much and attempt to swim? Did he kill himself, suddenly distressed by his infidelities? My thoughts swirled faster than the seagulls overhead.

"There you are." Tanner's voice sounded from behind me. I turned to see him walking briskly toward me. He sat down on the bench with me, wrapped his arm around my shoulder, and placed a tender kiss on my cheek.

"Good morning." I greeted him in a voice laced with irritation.

"Where'd you go? Don't disappear on me like that," he scolded.

"Sorry, I...I..." I didn't know what to say.

"It's fine. I'm glad you're okay. Are you okay?" He eyed me carefully.

"Yes." I scooched forward and his arm fell to the bench. "Thank you for asking."

"When I heard I raced here, but couldn't find you. I was worried." He rubbed my back, clearly oblivious to the don't-touch-me cues emanating from my pores. I stood up.

"Sorry to make you drive all this way. How were the roads in the storm?" My eyes burned into him. The number of people I could trust had recently plummeted dangerously close to zero.

"Not bad. The bridge was a bit backed up," he yawned.

Zero it is. My heart thumped indignantly in my chest, faster and faster with each passing second. I knew he was lying. There's no way he was in Belfast when I called him. No way he had to fight traffic on the bridge. It had taken him far less time to arrive. A crawling feeling slithered up my spine. He had been close by when I called him from the pier. I had assumed he'd tracked me somehow, but now I couldn't shake the feeling that he'd followed me here the night before. Was he stalking me? Isn't that what private investigators do though?

"I waited for you for a while but I couldn't be in the rain any longer," I lied, remembering I hadn't provided my location to him on the phone. Maybe I could confuse him now.

"I didn't see you, Macie. I'm sorry," he apologized.

"It doesn't matter," I backtracked. "I'm sorry I called you."

"Don't be." He stood up.

"Can I help you with something, Tanner?" I stepped back from him.

"What? No, I just..."

"What are you doing here?" I snapped, losing my cool as the events of the last few days suddenly caught up with me.

"I want to help," he pleaded.

"You're no longer my PI. I closed my account." I reminded him. I'd given him payment in full for his services the night we fucked. I still hated myself for being so vulnerable and needy. I despised other girls for being like that. I had two feet; I could stand on my own. I should stand on my own, but instead, I'd let him get me off balance. I'd let him distract me. Only once. And it hadn't been good. That was the one thing Michael excelled at: Sex.

I was never a priority for long, but when I was, it was always well worth it. Tanner had been, well, much like I'd expected. The good-looking guys usually are that way. There's not a lot of depth and depth was something I craved far more than physical attraction. Maybe I'd become grounded after Michael. Maybe I was just old school. I liked sex, don't get me wrong, but you have to at least like the person for the other twenty-three hours and forty-five minutes of every single day. It took more than a physical connection to accomplish that. I didn't have that connection with Michael. I hadn't been enough for him. I knew from the start I wouldn't be enough for him, but that's just how it goes sometimes.

"Macie..." Tanner stepped closer to me. I didn't back up. The truth was, I wanted someone's touch more than air right now. I needed to feel it on my skin. "Let me take you home," he whispered.

I nodded against my better judgment and let him lead me down the rose-lined park path to his truck. I let him open the door for me. I let him buckle my seatbelt, gently kissing my neck as he clicked it into place. I could almost feel myself click at the same time, giving in and surrendering my soul to this person I despised. I pretended to sleep while he drove me home to Belfast. I couldn't imagine stepping into my house, knowing Michael would never come home again. Perhaps a bigger part of me than I'd realized had hoped for reconciliation. Such a silly notion, that things could be mended. I must have drifted off to sleep because when I awoke, I was in a strange bed, in a strange room, alone.

"Hello?" I said, sitting up. The sheet drifted down my naked body. I shivered. "Tanner?"

No response. I got out of bed and walked to the window with the sheet draped around me. I pulled back the curtains to see the beautiful sights of the bay. We were practically over it, dangling in mid-air it seemed. I stretched and looked around. It was a plain bedroom, nice enough, sparsely decorated with photos of seashells and sand dunes. Just then the door opened, and Tanner walked in.

"Well good morning, sleepyhead," he chuckled from the doorway.

"Good morning," I replied.

"Would you like…" he started.

"Tanner, what am I doing here?" I interrupted him sharply. He took one step toward me, and I held my hand up to halt him. "I said take me home. This isn't home."

"This is my home." He took another step. "You were sleeping, and I thought…"

"You thought wrong," I hissed.

"Did I?" He quickly closed the gap between us, entangling his arms in the sheet that was now struggling to cover my nakedness.

I let him touch me. I let his fingers course through my hair and settle around my neck. I let my eyes flutter open at his command and I let him bite my lip, tipping my chin up to face him. It felt good to feel something else, to let my mind relax. I let him carry me back to the bed I'd just left, and I let him fuck me. I tried to concentrate on his touch, focusing on each individual sensation. From the way his fingers gripped my hips and ass, to the feel of his teeth on my skin, I let myself relish every pinch, every throb, every thrust. Then, in true Tanner fashion, it was over almost quicker than it began, and he left in search of coffee. I laid there feeling used, an easy target. I spotted my clothes in a pile on the floor, and I quickly dressed. As I slipped into Nadia's thong, I grinned. A full-fledged smile stretched from one side of my face to the other. I reached for my jacket and dug out Nadia's phone number, grateful I could still smile and grateful to see a smidge of hope in my very near future.

Twenty minutes later, I walked out of Tanner's door, slamming it so hard the glass shattered, much like my martini glass had done only a few days ago. I climbed into the backseat of Vince and Nadia's car and never looked back as we drove away.

THREE

"There are so many things that don't make sense," I said to Vince and Nadia as we sat together and sipped our coffees. They'd been gracious enough to pick me up and bring me back to Camden. I knew I had responsibilities and things I needed to deal with. Thankfully, the funeral preparations were being taken care of by Michael's parents, but there was still so much to do. I was stalling, sitting on the same bench where I'd sat earlier the day before, where Tanner had interrupted my life, claiming to want to help but being unable to follow through. Good riddance, I thought. I had managed to sleep though, for about twenty-four hours and my head felt clear again. I wanted to go to the store and purchase a new phone, but I didn't have the money. I needed to gather my belongings, including my car, and move on. Part of me didn't care if Tanner was tracking me. I didn't want him to have any power over me. I'd made my opinion of him very obvious when I slammed his door.

"Do you think he did it?" Nadia asked between bites of croissants.

"Did what?" I swallowed my extra dark mocha latte, forgetting how warm it was.

"Do you think he killed Michael?" she elaborated.

"Tanner?" I hadn't even thought of that, as crazy as it may seem.

"He seems almost obsessed with you," Nadia said quietly.

"No, you're right," I agreed.

"And he has the most to gain," Vince added.

"What's that?" I looked at him, confused.

"You."

Suddenly I felt nauseated. Waves of sickness threatened to ruin my delicious morning pastries. I hadn't stopped thinking about Annaleese long enough to consider anyone else. Maybe she was in town shopping during the hurricane. The weatherman had predicted a near miss, and truly we'd only gotten rain and a little wind. Not enough to close the shops. Camden housed some of the cutest shops in Maine. Belfast had shops too, of course, but Camden was superbly picturesque. You could shop and sip tea and feel like you belonged in a movie. It was all very quaint.

What if Tanner did kill Michael? It was plausible. Tanner had contingency plans mapping out what I should do if I ever needed him. If Michael ever got angry and hurt me, I was supposed to call Tanner. I remember the day we drew up the plans. I'd argued with him, assuring him Michael would never hurt me.

"Never underestimate how much people can surprise you," Tanner had said.

I remember his expression as he passed on his words of wisdom. Now, I felt icy cold thinking about it. Until yesterday I thought Tanner had a harmless crush. He was infatuated with me, for sure. That's all it was. But Tanner had a devilish streak, and I couldn't figure out why I always chose to ignore it. This wasn't something I could ignore. Was Tanner involved in my husband's death? Could he commit such a crime? Murder? I knew he was stalking me. I'd caught him lying several times now that I stopped to think about it. Was stalking just a teensy step away from murder?

"Fuck," I moaned, barely comprehensible. "I don't know what to think."

We sat for a while in silence. One by one many of the beautiful boats drifted out to sea. We watched as one of the fancy yachts on the left side of the cove lifted anchor and slowly floated away. I wanted nothing more than to float away with it. I could be a chef aboard a lovely vessel such as that, or a housekeeper even. I wanted a fresh start so badly.

Just then, two police officers approached our bench and stood directly in front of me, blocking my view of the disappearing yacht.

"Macie Black?" the one on the left asked.

"Yes?" I said, wondering if they'd found Michael's killer.

"You're under arrest ma'am, for the murder of Michael Black. Please stand up," he directed.

"What?" I heard Vince pipe up. I felt Nadia grab my hand as the officers guided me to a standing position. I heard them reciting my Miranda rights. I felt myself turn around and I felt the pinch of metal cuffs tightening around my wrists. I heard Nadia telling me not to worry, that everything would be fine. Then, standing in the tree line next to the library, I saw Tanner. He was watching, as always, this time his arms were folded gruffly across his chest. He nodded to me and smiled, clearly amused at my situation. I glared at him as the cops led me away.

Vick greeted me at the police station. I didn't speak. I couldn't say I was surprised they'd decided to throw the book at me. I was surprised they hadn't the first time around. Now Sergeant Renvick led me down a narrow hallway to what I assumed was another interrogation room. Instead, he opened the door to a small lounge, complete with a couch, small table, and coffee maker. The coffee maker sat on top of a small refrigerator no doubt stocked with water and creamer. I looked around for the two-way mirror but there wasn't one. Perhaps Camden needed to update their facilities, I thought. Vick closed the door behind us and removed my handcuffs.

"Mrs. Black…" he started.

"Macie is fine." I corrected him.

"Macie," he nodded. "I'm sorry for the disruption."

"I didn't do it. I already told you." I plead my innocence.

"I know. We know." Vick grabbed two bottles of water from the refrigerator.

"You know I'm innocent?" I asked, holding my breath for his response.

"Yes," he smiled at me. "Like I was saying, I'm sorry for the disruption, but we need to use you as bait."

"Bait?" I perked up. "So do you know who killed my husband?"

"We have our eyes on someone." Vick nodded.

"Who?" I asked, sitting on the edge of the sofa.

"Someone who has their eyes on you, Mrs. Black. We think this is a classic case of a jealous love triangle."

"A love triangle?" I gasped. "I told you she was involved!"

"Not Annaleese," he said. "Mrs. Black, what is your relationship with a Tanner Wilden, PI? Is he the private investigator you hired?"

"Yes," I swallowed hard. "He is. Why?"

"We have reason to believe he killed your husband."

"What?" I sat back, mortified. It was one thing for Vince and Nadia to wonder about Tanner's involvement, quite another thing for the police to say it. "Why arrest me then? He was there, you know? Watching me get arrested..."

"We know."

"So, you think you can get to him through me?"

"We're hoping," Vick paced the tiny room.

"What do you need me to do? Wear a wire?" I asked, ready to let Vick tape me up.

"It's a little more complicated than that." Vick clasped his hands behind his back and turned to me. "He's a smart man, an investigator, as you know. He'll find a wire."

"I just told him I never wanted to see him again," I admitted.

"That's fine. That's good!" Vince assured me.

"It is?" I was so confused.

"We believe him to be the type of man who won't take no for an answer," Vick explained. "He won't stop trying to get close to you."

I shivered. I knew he was right.

"Do you really think he killed Michael?" I didn't want to hear the answer.

"He killed him and dumped his body over a week ago." Vick watched me closely for my reaction. Seeing none, he elaborated. "A fishing vessel from Belfast was reported missing before the storm. It washed ashore just south of here after the hurricane. DNA scrapings from the vessel belong to Michael and Tanner. My guess is they tousled and only one man survived."

"But why?" My brain wouldn't work.

"With all due respect, Mrs. Black, you're gorgeous."

I didn't see myself as gorgeous. I thought I was pretty plain these days, but women are their own worst enemies when it comes to that. I sat there stunned as I replayed the last few months in my mind. I'd contacted Tanner out of desperation, not anger. I knew Michael was cheating, I just needed proof to let my mind rest. Tanner had seemed eager to take my case. He cleaned himself up after my initial visit. I remember thinking maybe I inspired him to get a haircut. We spent a lot of time together. I didn't have anything to compare the situation to, I just figured he was committed to the investigation. I was appreciative of his thoroughness. Now, I felt overwhelmed.

"But I served him papers." I reminded Sergeant Renvick as soon as the thought entered my mind.

"The prints on the envelope you gave your husband are not Michael's. They're Tanner's."

The tiny room began to spin. My heart raced. I thought back to about a week ago when I'd rushed into Tanner's office completely distraught. I'd been trying to reach Michael. The guilt of my indiscretion had been keeping me up at night, alone in our big house. It didn't make any sense. Michael was doing way worse to me, sleeping with countless women. Tanner had pictures of it all. But I wasn't like Michael. I wanted to talk to my husband, confess and hopefully make a plan to move forward. However, he wouldn't return my calls. Tanner held me while I cried. He convinced me to file for divorce. He said that way, Michael would have to react. A few days later, after countless unanswered phone calls, Tanner told me he located Michael at the hotel. I printed divorce papers immediately. I was outraged that the man I married couldn't be bothered to even return a text message; to at least let me know he was fine. I didn't stay at the hotel very long, seconds maybe, just long enough to pass him the envelope.

"Thanks, doll," he'd said.

Thanks, doll? Michael never called me doll. Tanner had several times. How could I not have seen what was right in front of me all this time? How could I have let him fool me, not to mention fuck me? I felt the bile rise in my throat and Vick handed me the trash can just in time. As I vomited, I tried to remember Michael's eyes that night, but I couldn't. I don't think I looked at his face. I was too distracted by his towel and the beautiful blonde woman on his arm. The door had been slammed in my face far too quickly to recall details.

"I'm sorry," I apologized, wiping my mouth with a tissue.

"Don't be," he empathized.

"Just to be clear." I felt the need to explain. "There is no love triangle on my part. I wasn't having an affair. Michael was. That's what started all this." My face flushed a deep red, maybe from the vomiting, but mostly from embarrassment.

"I'm sorry, Mrs. Black," he apologized. I again ignored his inability to call me by my first name.

"Am I under arrest or not?" I needed to get out of this stifling room.

"No, you're not, but we need to make it look like you are," Vick said.

"I'm listening," I replied and sat forward trying to do so.

"So far, the plan is going perfectly. In fact, your friends insisted on paying your bail already."

"Vince and Nadia?" I wondered out loud.

"Yes. We'll explain everything to them after, but it's perfect."

"Why's that?" I couldn't follow Vick's thought process.

"Because you can avoid jail. We need to make it look like you've moved on, like you're happy. Tanner won't like that. He'll resurface." Vick tried to catch me up to speed.

"Resurface? He was at the park. I told you that already." I could feel myself getting edgy.

"I mean he'll slip up. He'll do something to get you back, to draw you to him."

"I don't want my new friends in harm's way," I spoke up.

"You don't think they already are? He's seen you with them. They went to his house to pick you up this morning." Vick argued.

"How long have you been following me?" I asked angrily.

"With all due respect, Mrs. Black, your husband only died a few days ago," Vick snapped at me.

"I thought you said it'd been a week," I growled.

Sergeant Renvick sat back in his chair, unsure of what to say next. Thankfully, nothing else came out of his mouth. The tension was thick in the air around us. I felt like a fool.

"So, to backtrack..." I finally broke the silence. "You want me to pretend like I really got arrested, like they paid my bail, in hopes of irritating my husband's killer so he will come after me and then you will swoop in and arrest him?" It sounded like a mouthful and seemed like a million different things could go wrong, not to mention it was super unfair to Vince and Nadia who were only here on vacation. Surely, they wouldn't want to retire here now, with insanity lurking behind every idea. This plan was beyond ludicrous.

"I know you don't trust me." Vick stood and put the trash can just outside the door.

"Why can't you just arrest him now? Why do so many people need to be involved?" I pleaded for answers.

"He is a master of deception," Vick said slowly. "If he thinks we're onto him, he'll disappear. He'll go back to Boston. We don't think he knows about the stolen boat. We have a leg up on him. We need to catch him in the act."

"In the act of what?" I couldn't for the life of me figure out what the big issue was.

"We're waiting for a yacht to dock. It should have been here by now. We think the storm held it up." Vick continued mystifying me.

"A yacht?" I rubbed my forehead.

"Tanner meets this yacht every time it's here. We think he's laundering money out of it."

"So, there's a bigger issue here than my husband's murder? That's what you're saying?" I couldn't believe my luck. Out of all the private investigators out there, I'd chosen the most corrupt one by far. Now Michael's justice would have to wait. It infuriated me.

"Tanner Wilden is a worm," Vick's voice hinted at more than detest. "I know it's unfair to ask this of you, but we are hoping to take him down on both counts. We want to wipe the floor with him once and for all. We need your help."

"Tell me what you want me to do," I all but ordered Sergeant Renvick.

"We want you to get closer to him. Be with him. See if he'll let you into his world."

I stared at Sergeant Todd Renvick, my unblinking eyes blurring. After a few moments, my lips parted, and uncontrollable laughter erupted from them.

"Can I get you some coffee?" Vick asked, shifting uncomfortably in his seat as he spoke.

"Coffee?" My laughter slowly subsided. "You're going to have to do a lot better than coffee." My eyes penetrated his. I wondered what kind of man he was. Did he have a family? A wife? A daughter? Or was he more the type who only saw challenges, numbers, and re-elections? We stared at each other, neither one of us speaking, until he finally stood and left, closing the door behind him.

I stood up from the musty couch and paced the tiny room. From the door to the couch to the window, I walked in small circles, not even daring to think of anything except putting one foot in front of the other. Nadia would tell Vick to go screw himself, I was sure of it. I wanted to as well. A huge part of me thought this bordered on police brutality. How could they expect a grieving widow to behave in such a manner? On the other hand, Vick was offering me the sweet taste of revenge.

Thirty minutes passed before Vick walked through the doorway. He carried a paper bag from which he produced a bottle of Blue Barren Spiced Rum. I tried not to smile, to remain mad or at least appear to be mad. He poured us each a paper coffee cup of rum and sat down at the table. I sat down across from him.

"It's so funny." I took a sip. "When you're a kid you never think your life will turn out quite like this." I clinked my cup with his and quickly downed its contents.

"You are correct about that. We never expect what we get." He emptied his cup as well. "I always thought I'd be a cop, but here I am coercing you instead."

"What, they won't let you have a gun?" I attempted a joke.

"Oh, I have a gun," he chuckled. "But only one leg."

I looked down, not knowing what to say. He pushed his right leg out from under the table and pulled his pant leg up to reveal his prosthetic limb.

"I'm...I'm sorry," I muttered.

"Dirt bike accident, over twenty years ago now. I was a hot-headed teenager." He fixed his pant leg so it looked identical to the left one. "It's not so bad. I'm mostly bummed because it confines me to a desk."

"I never would have guessed." I let my voice trail off.

"It's certainly not what I expected." He winked at me and refilled our cups. I got the jist of his make-lemonade-with-lemons story.

"So, what exactly do I need to do?" I asked meekly. If he could rally his life after losing his leg as a teenager, I could carry on as well.

"We know it's unfathomable to ask, but we need you to get as close to him as possible. Hopefully, he'll bring you aboard the yacht sometime. It docks near the beginning of every month, except the winter months of course. He always exchanges two black duffle bags. We are so close to nabbing him, Macie."

So, he could use my first name.

"The only thing is you can't tell anyone what's going on. It's too much of a risk when we are this close. You can't tell Vince and Nadia," he advised.

"So, you're the only one who knows?" I felt afraid. I longed to talk to Nadia at least.

"Me and a handful of people here, on the inside. You can still have friends. Live your life. Just don't mention you are undercover."

"Live my life..." I stared into my sparkling amber drink.

"You'll be very generously compensated."

There it was: The cherry on top.

"Oh good," I said sarcastically.

"We suggest you go home, mourn Michael. Make any arrangements you need to. There are no restrictions other than please stay close. We can't, of course, pay you upfront. We can't leave a paper trail for Tanner to find. You understand." It was a comment rather than a question.

"And you're hoping...?" I wanted to make sure I understood the mission completely.

"If he doesn't contact you, which we are sure he will, reach out to him within the next few days. Apologize for getting angry, but make it look realistic."

"Of course." I rolled my eyes. "You think he'll apologize for killing my husband?"

"You can't tell him you know any of that," Vick admonished.

"I know," I snapped back. "Alright, well, we might as well get this show on the road." I stood up after I downed my drink again. "How do I reach you, in the event I need assistance?"

"Dial 911 and say, 'dirty green seal'. He couldn't even say it with a straight face.

"Dirty green seal?" I repeated.

"Yes. Dirty money in the ocean," he explained.

"How original," I murmured and opened the door to leave.

"Take care of yourself," he smiled at me.

"You too," I replied and walked back down the hallway to the front desk where I collected my cell phone, bag, and jacket. The woman glared at me like I was the enemy. Apparently, she wasn't in the inside circle.

Vince and Nadia were waiting for me on the benches outside the police station. They both rushed to my side when they saw me. Nadia hugged me like I'd just come home from war.

"Are you alright?" she asked, concern very evident in her voice.

"Yes, I'm fine," I lied. "Thank you both so much for bailing me out. You didn't have to do that."

"Don't mention it," Vince insisted.

I wanted to tell them they'd get their money back when this was all over, but I couldn't. Instead, I gave Vince a big hug. As I wrapped my arms around his broad shoulders, I recognized Tanner's truck in the parking lot. I looked from the truck body to the driver's side window and, sure enough, Tanner was sitting in the driver's seat.

FOUR

When I was a young girl, I dreamt of growing up and having a family. I wanted it all. One girl, one boy, one cat, one dog. All the standard American dream things. Growing up in Boston, everything was very accessible, just a plane ride, train ride, or taxi trip away. In fact, I didn't learn to drive until I came to Maine. I didn't need to drive. Not having a car meant not having to shovel around it or move it during winter storms. I didn't have to pay for tires or brake jobs or gas and insurance. Most of my girlfriends had cars so it was easy for me to find rides if I needed one.

Now, I sat in my car and stared out the windshield. I'd said goodbye to Vince and Nadia at the police station. They were uneasy about leaving me. They wanted me to return to Laconia with them.

They both had to work the next day and assured me I'd be comfortable in their home. I had no doubt I would be, but I could feel Tanner's eyes blazing into me, reminding me of my new priority. One I wished I could share with them, but I couldn't. I wanted to warn them, to tell them I was about to become an actress, but instead, I lied and told them Vick was giving me a ride home. I waved to them as they drove away. I waited for them to drive out of sight and I took a breath so deep I thought my lungs might burst.

I turned and walked to Tanner's truck. He rolled the window down but didn't get out. Tanner was always such a mystery. I silently wished I had a gun. I wished I could point it at his beady eyes and pull the trigger. I wouldn't even flinch. Instead, I leaned in close to him and let myself tear up.

"They think I did it." I started to cry. "They think I killed Michael." My sobs came harder and harder, and he opened his door to console me. I barely had to try, and I was in his arms.

"That's insane," he scoffed. "What about the blonde?"

"I don't know," I lied. "They're charging me. I can't leave the area." I let him hold me while I cried. If I closed my eyes I could almost pretend he was Michael. I hadn't realized how similar the two men were. Average build with tan complexions and strong arms; both men sported goatees and chiseled jawlines. Tanner did resemble Michael. How had I never noticed it before?

"Did they give you a radius?" Tanner asked, all business.

"I can't leave the Belfast, Camden, Rockland area," I sniffed.

"I see. Well, can I take you somewhere?" He tipped my chin up so he could look into my eyes. "Can I take you home?"

We'd played this silly game before, but I was in charge now. I held my cards close to my heart and replied, "Your home, please."

"Hop in." He tried not to smile.

I walked around to the other side of the truck and climbed inside. I asked him to take me to get my car, which was still in the parking lot at the end of Sea Street. I told him I'd follow him to his place. Now I stared out the windshield as I watched him drive away, knowing I had no choice but to follow him. Dancing with the devil was surely what I was doing now, no doubt about it. I followed him up US Route 1, past the Norumbega, past Camden Hills State Park, and countless bed and breakfasts, as well as charming antique shops. I drove slowly, not caring that I was holding up traffic. I knew what was in store for me when we arrived, and I hoped to prolong it as long as possible. The thought of Tanner's lips against my skin, his erection swollen inside me, had me wanting to hurl all over again. Could I do this? I was never good at faking anything. I usually wore my heart on my sleeve. I never had a good poker face, but I thought of Michael, fighting for his life on that boat because of me and my actions, and I knew I had no choice. I was the one who'd gotten Tanner involved. Now I would eliminate him if it was the last thing I did.

When we walked into Tanner's house, I was surprised to see the broken glass had already been replaced.

"I have a good carpenter buddy," he shrugged.

"I'm sorry," I lied yet again. I figured lying and I would become great friends by the time this charade was over.

"No, I'm sorry." He rubbed my arms. "I know you're grieving. I should have been more compassionate and showed more restraint. Please forgive me, Macie."

I didn't know what to say. He seemed so genuine. My belly growled loudly, saving me from having to reply.

"Why don't you take a nice warm bath while I cook dinner?" he suggested.

Dinner. Another day had disappeared faster than imaginable. As I peeled my clothes off and tossed them in the hamper, I realized I had been wearing the same thing for almost three days.

"Lovely," I whispered to the bubble bath waiting for me. I stepped into the warm water and let it soothe my soul. It felt amazing on my skin, almost as if it could heal me from the outside in. I squeezed the loofah and let the cleansing water drizzle over my shoulders. I had no idea what I was doing. No plan in sight. Vick had said I should just live my life, but I didn't know how to do that without Michael. I wished I could have left well enough alone. Things weren't bad with Michael. We could have agreed to see other people, a simple solution. I should have let it be, but I didn't and here we were.

Tanner knocked on the bathroom door, bolting me back to reality. There was no use in playing the 'what if' game now.

"Come in." I heard myself say.

Tanner stood in the doorway naked. The man clearly felt no shame.

"Can I wash your hair?" he asked.

I stared at him, this arrogant excuse of a man. Everything about him irked me. Must be a Taurus, I thought.

"Sure," my voice echoed throughout the bathroom.

I scooched forward in the bubbles, and he settled into the water behind me. He pulled me toward him, so I was lying between his knees, my head resting on his chest. He traced his hands up and down my arms, over my shoulders, and to my breasts where he paused to fondle each one. I felt him grow hard against my back and I cleared my throat.

"That's not my hair," I giggled. My giggle sounded strange to me like it belonged to someone else.

"My bad." He laughed and went about the job of wetting, washing, and rinsing my long full locks. To my pleasant surprise, when he finished he got out of the tub, dried himself off, and put on a pair of sweatpants.

It was starting to get dark out early now. Autumn would change to Winter soon. I stayed in the tub a while longer, watching darkness fall outside the small bathroom window. I thought of the big house Michael and I had called home. It would be very empty now. It was almost empty before. The four-bedroom, three-and-a-half-bath, colonial home had been a wedding gift from Michael's rich father. He didn't care for me but had to uphold his image for his son. With Michael gone, the house would likely default back to Gerald. I didn't want it anyway. I hadn't heard anything from either of Michael's parents. I had no idea when or if there'd be a service. Part of me wanted to inquire about it, to say my goodbyes to my first love, but I knew I wouldn't be welcome. We didn't get along, to say the least. Our personalities had always clashed. I wasn't a rich girl. I wasn't the right pedigree for their son. It was hard to believe, in today's progressive society, that people still felt that way. I remember laughing when Gerald pulled me aside after meeting him for the first time.

"Ain't no chance, sweet cheeks," he'd said.

"Excuse me?" I replied.

"You won't be anything but a fling. Michael knows what's expected of him." He warned me.

I'd rolled my eyes, giggling my foreign giggle. That's when Michael had approached, and conversation continued on into sports and news. I made it my mission from that moment on to become irresistible to Michael. He couldn't turn me away. I became everything he needed and wanted, allowing him the freedom to pursue his basketball dreams and the stability to feel secure and desired. Those were the good ole days, back before the wedding when I had everything to lose and the sole goal of proving Gerald wrong. And I had, but it hadn't changed his perception of me. I knew I would get the bare minimum, if anything, from Michael's death. A lot of it would depend on my undercover operation. The quicker we could wrap this up, the better. I was broke, and the public would be antsy, wondering who the Camden Harbor killer was.

Now, as I sat down to dinner with Tanner, I watched him pour me a glass of wine. I didn't know much about him. We'd grown up together but were never part of each other's lives. I didn't know his background or even what brought him to Maine. I didn't want to ask either, but I knew I needed to find a way to get closer to him.

"Thank you for being so nice," I said as I cut my steak. "It really means a lot to me."

"You're welcome." He lifted his glass. "To new beginnings."

My hand trembled as I touched my glass to his.

"Indeed." I grimaced inside but somehow managed to produce a smile.

We drank and talked and drank some more. I don't remember what we talked about, but I do remember I outdrank him. I had to. He was being so charismatic, so charming like maybe he knew I knew, but he was trying to get me to forget. That's all I wanted to do. Forget. Unfortunately for me, I had no such luck. I felt like Michael was there, watching us. I couldn't focus, couldn't breathe. Finally, I excused myself to use the bathroom. The image of the woman staring back at me in the mirror was a version I didn't recognize. I felt so lonely. I missed Nadia. I ached to talk to her. If I could just confide in her, I was sure everything would be alright. As soon as I convinced myself to call her, I talked myself out of it. Tanner had to go down. He had to pay for his crimes. There was no turning back now. So, I did the only thing I could think to do.

I walked back to the kitchen where Tanner was still sitting at the table. I took a deep breath, bit my bottom lip, and went to stand beside him. I untied the robe I was wearing and let it fall open and off my shoulders. He sat back in his chair and groaned as his eyes scanned my body. I wasn't skinny, but I wasn't big either, an average size, I suppose. My body curved in all the right places, my breasts ample and perky, a bonus to never having children. My long legs accentuated my slender hips, making me appear taller than I was. I stood before him and pushed our dishes to the other end of the rectangular wooden table. Then I lifted myself to sit in front of him, my open legs straddling him unapologetically.

"I'm tired of talking," I said in the dimly lit room.

He looked at me intently but didn't say a word. His big hands started at my feet and slowly slid their way up each leg and around to my inner thighs. I tossed my head back, my chin facing the chandelier. He stood up and pushed his chair back. It fell against the linoleum floor. Then he was kissing me, his lips bruising against mine. His firm touch brought tears to my eyes, a very welcome distraction. His fingers felt my nipples and twisted hard, sending stinging sensations throughout my entire body. I finally felt myself begin to relax as I retreated into a cloud of passion and utter betrayal. To let Michael's killer fuck me was one thing; but to enjoy it, to get lost in his touch, was something entirely different. Like I said, there was no turning back now.

The next day, sure enough, Tanner received a call and had to go out for a few hours. I had no idea who called. He always kept his phone close by and always excused himself to answer it. I understood, for the most part. His career was one of secrets. I never asked questions. I did, however, watch him through the lace curtains as he unlocked the backyard shed and brought out two black duffle bags. He put them in the backseat of his truck and drove away. I sunk to the floor where I'd been standing and sat with my head in my hands. How was it possible for life to change so dramatically in such a short amount of time? Less than a week ago my life, while less than perfect, was a thousand shades different than it was now. I pulled myself up off Tanner's dusty floor and decided now was a good time to go to my own house and see what awaited me there.

Michael and I lived on Church Street, just a few blocks away from Tanner's hip waterfront home. I hadn't even thought it to be at all consequential when Tanner said he lived so close to me. On the contrary, I thought it was convenient. Now I questioned how long he'd been there and what brought him to Belfast in the first place. He didn't have an office front here, like most businesses did. He always met people out and about. We met for the first time at Heritage Park in the gazebo. It seemed like a good place to size each other up but not be alone. I didn't trust Tanner from the beginning. I needed to learn to obey my instincts.

I pulled up to my garage and parked next to Gerald's blue Mustang. I took a deep breath and walked up my stone walkway to the front door. I was hoping to be alone here, but not at all surprised when Gerald opened the door and stood in the way, blocking my entrance.

"Gerald," I said, refusing to call him Mr. Black as he requested.

He didn't speak, didn't move, just glared at me. I stepped up so I was level with him, and he slowly moved out of the way. That's when I noticed he'd been crying. His son was dead, after all. Though Gerald had never liked me, he and Michael had been quite close. I didn't say anything else to him and thankfully he walked out of the house, closing the door quietly behind him, and drove away. I breathed a sigh of relief, happy to have a solitary moment to myself.

The house looked the same as it had when I left. It was far too fancy for my taste, complete with a formal sitting room and study. We never studied. Perhaps if I had studied to begin with, all those years ago as a college freshman, I'd be in a completely different world now, dealing with animals instead of humans. Funny how life is nothing but a series of decisions all strung together, each choice bumping up against the next, begging for acceptance. I peeked into the dining room and kitchen as I passed by. Except for the pile of mail on the kitchen table, nothing appeared to be out of place. Gerald must not have been here long.

I walked into the bedroom and laid down on the bed that Michael and I had bought together. He had wanted a four-poster, dark, oak bedroom set and since it was his money, that's what we purchased. He'd teased me at the time, making the clerk blush as he promised to tie me to the posts. I smiled at the memory and then, as if my heart couldn't handle any more emotion, tears began to cascade down my cheeks. My entire body shook as I finally mourned my husband, a man I had at one time loved with every fiber of my being. To think that people were assuming I killed him, that I'd reached my limit and lashed out, that I'd come to the end of my rope, seemed like a bad joke. Yes, I'd been frustrated with Michael at the end, but I'd never kill someone. Well, maybe Tanner.

I stood up at the thought of Tanner and tore at my clothes. I pulled my shirt over my head and threw it into the corner of the room, then my pants and socks. My bra followed and then Nadia's thong. I'd worn my dirty clothes because I didn't want to run into Gerald while I was wearing Tanner's sweatpants. My clothes were in desperate need of laundering. I walked into our master bathroom and started the shower. I didn't wait for the water to get hot. I stepped into the cold shower, praying that the droplets would wash away my sins, cleanse my body, and rid me of the filth I felt so deeply. The water turned hotter, and I scrubbed at my skin as if a good shower would help my situation. When I was finished, I shut the water off and dried my body, but my face remained wet, unstoppable tears still streaming from my eyes. Finally, I wrapped a towel around my body and sat down in the overstuffed chair in front of my bedroom window.

Our house was white with black shutters, a classic old Maine house. It had been renovated prior to us moving in, compliments of Gerald. I used to like sitting in this chair and watching the quiet street below. That is until Michael stopped coming home every night. I'd sit up waiting for him, sitting in this chair, no lights on, hoping to see his headlights pulling in the driveway. Now I sat in the chair, knowing he would never come home again. Irritation and anger slowly began to replace my sadness, bringing me back to the here and now. At this moment, I was supposed to be packing my belongings. I didn't want to have to run into Gerald again. I opened my closet door and pulled my suitcases down from the shelf. I packed my clothes and personal items, including all my toiletries and items in the small desk in the corner of the room. Next, I walked through the other upstairs bedrooms, like I knew I'd never be back. Then I walked down the stairs and left my bags by the side door.

I slowly paced through each room, grabbing any items I wanted, which wasn't much. A few throw pillows, a blanket with our pictures printed on it that we'd received as a wedding present, and a few knick-knacks, souvenirs of our time together. I put my things in my car and did a quick scan of the garage. Seeing nothing I wanted, I went into the house and sat at the kitchen table to go through the pile of mail. I sifted through the pile of standard household letters; fliers with coupons, credit card offers, and such. Three-quarters of the way through the stack, a small yellow envelope caught my attention. It didn't have a return address and I didn't recognize the font. I slid my finger under the crease at the top and ripped the pale yellow envelope open. Inside was a blank sympathy card with a sketched picture of a hummingbird on the front. It simply read:

'I'm Sorry - Annaleese'

I dropped the card on the table and wiped my contaminated fingers on my pants. I didn't want her apologies. I didn't want to think of her as human. She must be grieving too, or at the very least feeling the pangs of guilt that any decent woman would feel after helping to break up a marriage. I knew her role in my marriage's demise was quite minuscule, but after reading her sympathy card, I'm guessing she didn't realize that. I picked the card up again and studied it carefully, as well as the envelope. No return address and no phone number, but it was postmarked right here in town. I wondered for a brief moment how she knew my address, but it didn't matter. Nothing mattered now. I picked up the entire pile of mail and threw it in the trash, including Annaleese's card. I did one last quick walkabout of the house where Michael and I had lived for the last seven years. Seeing nothing else I wanted, I took my house key off my keychain and left it on the kitchen table. I walked to the front door, turning around only once to blow a kiss to our wedding photo that was situated directly above the mantle. Then, with one foot in front of the other, I walked to my car and drove back to Michael's killer's house.

FIVE

The first few nights at Tanner's, I slept like a baby. I couldn't get over how exhausted I was. Life toppling upside down can take a lot out of a person. I didn't do anything except sleep, eat, and pretend to enjoy Tanner's touch. He seemed to be on Cloud Nine. I'd hoped to be home before him on the day he left with the duffle bags, but he was already back when I arrived. He met me at the door with a guarded expression on his face like he didn't approve of me going anywhere without his consent, but when he saw that I had luggage and decorative throw pillows, his mood lightened. We hadn't discussed me moving in, but here I was, following him to the bedroom with my suitcases. He was beaming. I fought back the urge to throw up. I'd learned a trick of breathing in deeply and slowly while touching my tongue to the roof of my mouth. Maybe it was all in my head, but it seemed to prevent me from vomiting so that's what I did.

"I can bring another dresser in here for your things," Tanner suggested.

I smiled appreciatively at him, and he ran down the hall to the spare bedroom. I opened his closet door to grab a coat hanger and my attention was immediately drawn to the floor. A pair of boots had been hastily tossed there and they appeared to have blood caked on them. I quickly shut the door and turned back to my suitcases. Every ounce of me wanted to run, to leave all my shit behind and just run. I could run as fast as I could and call Vince and Nadia. They would rescue me. I could start over in Laconia. Tanner came back into the room, dragging a dresser behind him. He was all smiles. It made me sick. I knew he couldn't get away with this, so again, I took a deep breath and continued unpacking.

"Do you have room in your closet if I hang a few things?" I asked innocently.

"Um, I think so," he scratched his head.

"Do you want a drink? I could use a drink?" I yawned.

"Sure," Tanner chirped excitedly, "I'll take a beer."

"I'll be right back," I exited the bedroom and paused just out of sight. I could see him in the mirror, as he rushed to the closet and picked up the boots. He twirled around for a moment, no doubt wondering where he would put the incriminating evidence, and then I watched as he stuffed them under the bed.

I continued to the kitchen, knowing I needed to somehow up my game. I needed him to bond with me on a nonsexual level. It was the last thing I wanted, to bond with Michael's murderer, and I didn't have any idea how to go about doing it. Sex was easy. This... well, this seemed downright impossible.

I think that's why I couldn't sleep at night. Once the stillness of the night blanketed us with its eeriness, all I could do was rack my brain trying to figure out how to get Tanner to open up. None of my ideas seemed like they'd work. This was harder than I'd imagined it would be. Hard because my heart wasn't my own. It was someone else's. Someone who was living the life of a widow, playing along with the hand she was dealt, but it didn't feel like me. I wasn't allowed to mourn or grieve unless I was alone. I wanted Tanner to think I was falling in love with him, and I couldn't do that if I was still hung up on Michael's death.

Two weeks after I moved in with Tanner, I finally got a break. He was headed back to Boston to see his family for the weekend. He asked if I minded if he went alone, which surprised yet pleased me at the same time. I watched him leave, expecting him to go to the backyard shed first but he did not. Perfect, I thought, because I wanted to snoop. I wanted to see what was in the bags because if it wasn't money, if it was something silly like clothes or canned goods, I would jump ship on this undercover investigation so fast it would make my own head spin. I would get the bloody boots from under the bed where I slept with this murderous man every night and I would take them to Sergeant Renvick and demand Tanner's immediate arrest.

I would cause such a fuss, taking my story to the news outlets if I had to. I wanted nothing more than to see Tanner Wilden behind bars.

I stepped out Tanner's back door intending to break into his shed, but something stopped me. What if he had cameras in there? A private investigator had a knack for cameras. I knew I shouldn't chance it; I could blow the whole thing. I stood on the back porch and let the tears fall down my cheeks yet again. I sank to my knees on the splintery wood and tried to gain control over my shaking body. Finally, I stood up and went back inside. I lay down on the couch and drifted off to sleep.

An hour or so later I was woken by a car door shutting. I laid still on the couch, wondering who could be visiting or if Tanner had changed his mind about going away for the weekend. A few seconds passed and there was no knock, no footsteps, nothing. I slowly stood up and looked out the window. There was a gray midsize car in the driveway, but there didn't appear to be anyone in it. I walked to the window and still didn't see anyone. I walked to the back door and saw blonde hair bouncing away as someone hurried to the shed. I sank as low as possible so I could still see but not be seen and I watched as a woman opened the shed door and emerged with one black duffle bag. She backed out, so I couldn't see her face, locked the door behind her, and walked back to her car. I rushed to the front door, hoping to catch a glimpse of her face and then my heart stopped beating completely. Annaleese climbed into her car and drove away.

I stood there dumbfounded. Perhaps Michael's murder had been a crime of passion; a threesome gone very wrong. Was Michael in on this washing money scheme too? Did the three of them have a side business no one else knew about? What was the real reason Michael was killed? Suddenly I knew what I had to do, and it wasn't to stay here alone for the weekend. I ran upstairs and packed a small bag with a change of clothes, then I drove to Camden and checked into the same hotel I had stayed in before.

Saturday morning, I lay in my comfy hotel bed contemplating getting a muffin and coffee and going to the park for a while. I loved it there. Watching the boats was soothing to my soul. Since Michael's death, I felt like the harbor was calling to me, beckoning me to visit. I assumed it was because this was the last place I saw Michael, albeit not alive. But this trip wasn't a social visit. I got out of bed and readied myself for the morning. I dressed in a respectable, shin-length, navy blue dress and my favorite platform sandals. We were having an Indian summer here in Maine, post-hurricane, which didn't help mellow my desire to go to the park.

At eight o'clock on the dot, I walked through the doors of the Camden Police Station. The same grumpy woman as before failed to greet me. I didn't care. I sauntered past her desk like I owned the place, my hips swaying slightly as I careened down the hallway to Sergeant Renvick's office.

"Excuse me, ma'am? Ma'am!" The cranky receptionist noticed me now. I tossed my hair from one shoulder to the other, a petty form of acknowledgment, and I knocked quickly before entering Vick's office. He was finishing up a phone call and motioned for me to take a seat. I remained standing, impatiently tapping one finger against my purse strap. When his conversation didn't appear to be wrapping up, I laid my index finger on the telephone, swiftly ending his call.

"Good morning, Mrs. Black," he sighed and hung up the receiver. "What can I do for you today?"

"We need to chat." I shifted my weight from one foot to the other.

"Alright." He got up and shut his office door.

"Did you know she was in on this too?" I spattered.

"Who?" He sat back down in his leather chair and took a granola bar out of his desk drawer.

"Annaleese," I hissed and reached across his desk, snatching away his breakfast.

"Really?" He seemed genuinely surprised.

"She was at the house this morning, Tanner's house. She took a black duffle bag from the shed." I finally sat down and tossed his granola bar at him. He didn't catch it. It bounced off his chest and landed on the floor.

"Are you sure it was her?" His question was offensive in my ears.

"Yes," I said very slowly.

Sergeant Todd Renvick put both hands behind his head and stared up at the stained ceiling tiles.

"You didn't know," I whispered. "Bitch even sent me a sympathy card."

"What?" He sat forward in his chair.

"Why is it that men never think the blonde girls are guilty?" I laughed.

"She sent you a card?" He asked, making sure he'd heard me right the first time.

"It didn't say much, just 'I'm sorry' and her name." I rolled my eyes.

"She sent you a handwritten card?" Vick clarified, his interest obviously peaked.

"I know, right? How lame," I rolled my eyes again.

"Do you still have it?" he asked.

"No. I threw it in the trash." I looked at him like he was crazy. Why on earth would I want to keep such a thing?

"Shit," he grumbled.

"Why?" I asked, confused.

"Well, if we knew what her handwriting looks like it could be a game changer," Vick explained.

Duh. I hadn't even thought of that. I would make a very bad detective.

"If you have something to compare it to, I'm sure I could easily recognize her writing," I suggested, remembering her font had been quite original.

"Actually…" Vick sat straight up in his chair and started rummaging around on his computer. I watched his eyes dart back and forth as he looked at the screen. "Tanner has an offshore bank account and, if I remember correctly, the signature on the deposit slips was unique. Ah, yes, right there. Come look at this." He pointed to the screen.

I stood up and walked around Vick's desk so I could see what he was referring to. Sure enough, the black font scribbled out on the screen matched Annaleese's.

"Yup," I nodded my head. "That's it. That's her writing."

"Macie!" Vick's voice changed to excitement. "You are incredible! Great work! We couldn't figure it out. That was a big missing puzzle piece!"

"Wonderful!" I said. "I'm glad, but what do I do now?"

"Keep doing what you're doing," Vick encouraged. "In fact, try to get close to her too."

"Her?" I looked at him like his head was two sizes too small. "Annaleese?"

He started to nod but stopped halfway through. I laughed at him. I knelt, picked up his chocolate chip granola bar, and placed it on his desk before walking briskly out of the room. A second later I popped my head back through his doorway.

"You should probably see if Michael is connected to any of this." I shrugged and then turned to leave.

Later that evening as the sun set behind Mount Battie, I snuggled comfortably in my hotel bed and stared out the window at the ever-changing colors of the sky. I'd eaten an early dinner at Cuzzy's and was looking forward to my relaxing evening alone. Bubble baths had lost their appeal, so I took a long hot shower and tried my best to reset my brain. I had almost convinced myself for the seventeenth time, to walk away from it all when suddenly there was a knock on the door. I hopped out of bed to answer it and my heart stopped when I saw Tanner's face through the peephole.

"Macie, it's me. Open up." Tanner knocked a second time.

"Tanner," I said, opening the door. "What are you doing here? Are you following me?"

"You paid for the room with my credit card," he reminded me. "I got a text alert."

Goddamn technology, I'd forgotten about that. He'd been generous enough to give me one of his credit cards and I hadn't thought twice about using it. I wouldn't make a good fugitive either, that was for sure.

"It's fine. It's okay," he assured me. "I just wanted to check on you. I don't have to stay." He seemed to be more understanding than usual, and I wondered for a brief moment, if Annaleese saw me at the house. Then, for another brief moment,

I wondered if he knew Annaleese was there to begin with.

"I'm sorry," I mumbled. "The house was so lonely without you. Wait, what are you doing back already?"

"I missed you." He swallowed hard. Too hard; his Adam's apple clearly covering a lie. For a private investigator, he didn't cover his tracks very well. Or was it just because I knew how guilty he really was?

"I'll go," he cleared his throat.

"No," I tugged on his sleeve. "Please, stay."

This lying game was becoming very natural to me, comfortable even, especially when I was able to view it as a job. If I gave up now, I'd never be rid of Tanner. That was the one thing I knew for certain.

SIX

As the weather grew colder with each passing day, I began to feel paranoid that this case would never be wrapped up by winter. The yachts didn't sail in the cold winter months and the thought of being cooped up with Tanner from December to April more than made my skin crawl. We were getting along great; everything was going very well, but I wasn't making much progress, and pretending with Tanner was exhausting.

Michael's parents decided to cremate him, specifically so I couldn't visit his grave, I'm sure. As much as it broke my heart to leave things unresolved, I held on to the fact that there was nothing I could do about it now. Fate had already chosen for me. It had almost been one month since Michael's death. November was fast approaching. The trees were mostly bare now, waiting for snowflakes to cover them in white.

One sunny afternoon, as I shuffled from job interview to job interview, I received a phone call from Michael's mother, Bonnie. I didn't answer it, of course. I stared at the screen until the notification appeared that she'd left a voicemail. My fingers had a life of their own as they hit the play button. Bonnie sounded desperate to see me. Somewhere neutral, somewhere not in Belfast or Camden. I must have replayed the message at least twenty times, each time trying to gauge the haughtiness in her voice, but for the first time, she sounded more worried than arrogant.

I decided my interview at the bank wasn't nearly as important as meeting her. I waited as long as I could, about five minutes, before texting her to meet me at the Rockland Breakwater. You might think that's a poor choice for a meeting place, what with all the slippery rocks, but there were benches there too, and water her son hadn't bobbed around in.

It takes approximately ten minutes to drive from Camden, Maine to Rockland, Maine. It is eight miles as the crow flies, more like eight and a half if you are driving on Maine's classic US Route 1. The road, which is described as a historical and scenic drive, stretches from Fort Kent, Maine to Key West, Florida. As I passed the sign welcoming me to Rockland, I wanted nothing more than to keep driving straight to Key West. I could live a simple life down there, on a canal with a pet manatee, and no worries. I knew that was nothing more than a fantasy. As I turned left at the sign for the Samoset Resort, I watched in my rearview mirror as a white SUV followed me. I knew it was Bonnie, I could see her fancy sunglasses through the windshield.

I parked in the lot designated for the Breakwater and waited while she parked next to me. I took a deep breath and started to get out of my car when she knocked on my passenger side door. I unlocked it, and she climbed in.

"I don't think anyone followed me," she stated.

"Hi, Bonnie," I greeted her cautiously.

"Hi yourself," she snipped. Yup, she was still her lovely self.

"Bonnie, I'm so very sorry..." I started to offer my condolences, but she put her hand up in the air between us to silence me.

"I'm not sure what you kids were into." She glared at me from behind her shades. "And I don't want to know. But you have to take these bags. I don't know where they came from, or why Michael had them in his room, but you take them. I'm sure you know."

With that, she got out of the car, opened my back door, as well as hers, and tossed five big black duffle bags into my innocent little Subaru. She didn't look at me again, didn't say another word, just got back in her SUV and drove away.

I sat there stunned, staring at the black bags that were now strewn about my back seat. I didn't want to touch them. I didn't want my fingerprints on them, but I had to know, so I carefully unzipped one corner. Sure enough, stacks of banded money filled the bag. I twisted around in my seat to inspect them. Hundreds of thousands of dollars, millions perhaps, floated around in my backseat.

"Fuck!" I screamed out loud in my car. "Fuck! What am I supposed to do with all this?" I had nowhere to hide this money, nowhere to even call my own. Funny, to be beyond completely broke and fall into all this money. The temptation to take it and run gnawed at my entire being. Instead, I put my car in drive and drove.

***

Sergeant Renvick walked out of the police station, heading nonchalantly to my vehicle. I backed in between two police cruisers. He walked to my door, and I rolled my window down only a little, enough so he could hear me tell him to get in. He rolled his eyes at me and made his way to the passenger door.

"What is it?" he asked a bit grumpily. "I'm right in the middle of something."

"Funny," I sneered. "Me too." I nodded to my backseat full of duffle bags.

"Macie!" Vick exclaimed, clearly astonished. "What did you do?"

"I didn't do anything!" I touched my left hand to my chest like the gesture would solidify my innocence.

"Where'd you get these?" He unzipped the corner of one bag, just like I'd previously done. Stacks and stacks of money greeted him too.

"Michael's mother threw them in my car about twenty minutes ago." My voice was laced with indignation.

"Oh, Macie," Vick whispered. "This is bad. This is very, very bad."

"I know!" I chuckled. "Now I'm in as deep as everyone else; smeared by whatever the fuck is actually going on."

"Did anyone follow you here?" He shifted in his seat.

"I don't think so," I shrugged.

"We can't just carry them inside right here in plain daylight," Vick looked around nervously.

"That's not why I came here. I'm keeping the bags. I just wanted you to see them," I explained.

"You're keeping the bags?" He raised one eyebrow and stared at me. "Macie, you can't just keep them. This is dirty money."

"I know it's dirty money!" I hissed. "I'm going to give the bags to Tanner."

Vick didn't say a word, so I continued.

"Listen, I can't do this anymore. Things are stagnant. I'll give him the bags, I'll tell him they came from Michael's mother, and I'll tell him I want in on whatever's going on. This will either earn me a ticket to the front door of that yacht or..."

"Or he'll kill you." Vick finished the equation.

"Well, at least we'll be heading in a direction. Honestly, Vick, I can't stay with him all winter. We need to wrap this up. Clearly, Michael was a part of this. Bonnie said she found the bags when she was cleaning his room."

"His room, where?" Vick grabbed his skinny spiralbound notebook out of his jacket pocket and started jotting down information.

"His room at her house, where he grew up in Vinalhaven."

"His parents are separated, correct?" Vick asked.

"Yes. His dad lives in Belfast. His mom still lives on the island."

"Oh, okay, that makes sense. I'd like to bring her in for questioning, but she can't know you're working with us. Sometimes I wonder..." his voice trailed off.

"You wonder what?" I pressed him.

"How well do you know Gerald?"

"Mr. Gerald Black?" I rolled my eyes. "He is a treat."

"We wonder if the yacht might be his. Those bags being at Michael's mother's, make me wonder even more."

"For sure." I rubbed my forehead. I could feel a migraine brewing. "It wouldn't surprise me. Can't you look up who owns it?"

I'd done that several times over the years. Google always held the answers. I'd see gorgeous yachts floating in the harbor and look up their names online. They were always owned by important rich people or celebrities.

"We've looked. It's deeded to a lie. It's true ownership hidden behind a bogus corporation." Vick looked out the window, agitated.

"Seems like a Gerald thing to do." I nodded.

"But would he kill his son?" Vick's question sent shivers up my spine. "And the mother had no idea what the bags were from?"

"She didn't seem to," I said, ignoring Vick's first question altogether.

"Interesting." He tapped his pen on his notepad.

"Listen, I'm just going to run with this. I'm going to give these bags to Tanner and see where it goes."

"What about Annaleese? Anything new with her?" Vick asked.

"No," I said curtly.

"Alright, alright." He held his hands up in surrender. "What do you need from me?" He turned and snapped a few pictures of my backseat full of loot.

"Just that," I said. "I wanted you to see the bags so you can corroborate my story."

"Smart thinking. You'd make a good detective, Macie," he smiled.

I smiled back at him, letting his words resonate in my soul. *It's never too late to start a new career,* I thought.

***

As I drove back to Tanner's house, I couldn't get Vick's words out of my mind. As much as this case boiled my blood, it did intrigue me. Undercover work is not for the faint of heart. I'd learned that lesson up close and personal. I was lost in my own world, dreaming of becoming a detective, when I drove right past her. I didn't notice her at first, surely a good detective would have noticed. I slowed down and turned around in the next driveway, quickly retreating to where I'd seen the blonde girl limping down the side of US Route 1.

I pulled onto the shoulder of the road and called out her name.

"Annaleese?" I hollered.

The woman stopped walking, turned, and stared at me. Her bottom lip was split open and bleeding. Her right temple was gashed to match her lip. She couldn't open one eye; it was swollen shut. Blood was caked to the side of her head, matted into her usually bouncing blonde curls.

"Annaleese!" I threw my car in park and ran to her. She almost buckled when I put my arm around her. "Come on," I said. "Let's get you out of here."

Without thinking about the bags of money in my backseat, I opened the front passenger door and helped her climb inside. Her right knee was swollen to the size of a soccer ball. Someone had done a number on her.

I sped back to Camden, wishing I could call Sergeant Renvick, but knowing I couldn't. I wouldn't blow my cover.

"Annaleese?" I spoke loudly, hoping she wasn't passed out. "Annaleese, who did this to you?"

She moaned but didn't speak.

"Annaleese?" I tried again but received no reaction. "Was it Tanner?" I couldn't help but ask the incriminating question. "Annaleese, I know you know Tanner."

Sobs shook her entire body, and I had my answer.

SEVEN

If you're lucky, calling 911 is something you don't have to do in your lifetime. It sticks with you, making that phone call. No matter the reason. Maybe it's the adrenaline rush that usually accompanies the moment. As I rushed Annaleese to the hospital, I knew exactly what my next step would be. Enough was enough. This rolling snowball was picking up speed faster than I could keep up with alone. And now I wasn't alone. Now it was Annaleese and I against them. Whoever 'them' was...

I pulled up to the sliding glass door of the emergency room and left my car in park while I rushed Annaleese inside. I wasn't inside even five minutes, but when I went back out to move my car, it was gone. I looked around, thinking maybe I'd been blocking the entrance and someone moved it out of the way. No such luck. I twirled in frantic circles, only making myself dizzy, not fixing anything. I paused to try to pull myself together, and then I walked back through the automatic doors and told the balding security guard that someone had stolen my vehicle.

Of course, my phone was in my bag in my car. I knew in my gut this was no coincidence. This was all part of the bigger scheme at hand. I asked the officer if I could use the telephone and he kindly directed me to a desk. I picked up the phone and dialed 911. When the operator asked for the state of my emergency, I said, 'dirty green seal' and was promptly redirected.

"Renvick." The voice on the other end greeted me.

"I'm at the hospital with Annaleese," I said sharply. "Tanner assaulted her. Oh, and in the two minutes I was helping her inside, someone stole my car, complete with all its contents."

"You've had a busy afternoon," Vick commented. "I'll be right there."

I hung up the phone just in time to race down the hallway after Annaleese's gurney.

"Ma'am! Ma'am, you can't go back there." An orderly stopped me. "They're taking her for tests. She'll be back shortly. You can wait in her exam room."

I nodded slowly and the person dressed in pale blue scrubs led me down the corridor. Once inside, I paced the tiny room. It was split in two sections, divided by a gray curtain hanging from a ceiling track. There were no windows. As I paced, the room got smaller and smaller; the walls closing in on me until I had no choice but to sink to the laminated floor. I sat there, pulling my knees up to my chin, my fingers interlaced around them in a white-knuckled grip.

A few moments later, the curtain flung open, and Vick entered. He raced to my side; my ghostly appearance clearly scaring him.

"Macie, Macie, are you okay?" He helped me to my feet with the assistance of a nearby nurse. I sat in a chair and the nurse handed me a drink of water.

"I'd say things are escalating!" I whispered aggressively after the nurse left.

"I was afraid of this," Vick responded.

"I didn't mind the danger when it was just me." I shook my head. "He beat the shit out of her!"

"What happened, exactly?" He leaned back against the wall.

"I was almost halfway back to Belfast when I saw her limping down the shoulder of the road. I turned around and picked her up. It was awful. She could barely walk. She could only see out of one eye, and her face..." I paused before continuing. "It was bad."

"So, you brought her in here and when you went back to your car, it was gone? And you're sure no one moved it?"

"I'm sure," I nodded.

"Did she see the backseat?" he asked.

"No," I assured him. "She could barely see at all."

"And she said Tanner did it?"

"I asked her if he did it and she burst into tears," I explained.

"Oh," he replied.

"Oh? Oh, what?" I inquired.

"Well, she didn't physically say it?" He started pacing.

I didn't respond. I stared up at him from the vinyl hospital chair. I knew he knew what I was thinking, even though I lacked the actual words to say it.

"Macie, I'm sorry." He held his hands up. "I know the system is broken, but if she didn't say the words..."

"I'm done with this!" I stood up, exasperated. "I'm done! I don't want anything else to do with this!"

"You can't just..." He started to lecture me, but I interrupted him.

"You know he killed my husband! You know he's laundering money! You know, as well as I do, he assaulted that girl, yet you're doing nothing! Well, you know what else? I don't care anymore! My husband didn't die a victim. He died a cheating bastard. He died a criminal. I say good riddance! I don't need vindication any longer and I certainly don't need whatever the fuck this is!"

I turned to walk away, to escape this utter mess that had become my life, and I almost ran directly into Annaleese's gurney as it wheeled back into the room. I jumped back to get out of the way and bumped into Vick's leg, causing him to lose his balance. I grabbed a hold of him, holding his hand in mine while I steadied myself.

"I'm sorry," I whispered, resisting the urge to cry; to break into a million shattered pieces right here in front of this kind man.

Annaleese was awake, struggling to see us out of her one working eye. She held her hand out to me and I couldn't not go to her. I heard Sergeant Renvick introduce himself to the doctor and ask for an update.

"She has a severe concussion, several broken ribs, a broken nose and jaw, and a broken knee cap. She's subdued right now, because of the morphine. She's a very lucky lady. Someone worked her over good."

"Lucky?" I grunted, disheveled at his comment.

I felt Annaleese squeeze my hand and I knew I couldn't leave now. I couldn't abandon her like this, in this condition of raw frailty. I felt Vick's eyes on me. I looked up to give him a reassuring nod before he stepped out into the hallway with the doctor, likely to discuss the dirty deeds that no one wants to discuss in front of a woman. Was she raped? Was there evidence of a struggle? Yes, and yes, were my immediate assumptions.

When Sergeant Renvick came back in the room, he looked more worried than when he'd left. His face told stories his lips did not and the next thing I knew, we were being relocated to a private room with actual walls and windows. Two uniformed police officers with guns were placed outside the door, as a precaution Vick said, but I knew it was more than that. I knew Tanner was guilty when he didn't come to tell me he wasn't. I knew he had stolen my car. Vick put a BOLO out of my stylish yet classic Subaru and within minutes it was spotted in a lower parking lot near the pier. The bags in the backseat were nowhere to be seen. Somehow Tanner must have known I had the bags. I couldn't quite get the puzzle pieces to lock into place. The tricky part, the part that became more and more muddled in my brain, was that Tanner couldn't be in two places at once. There was no way he followed me to the Breakwater and saw Bonnie put the bags in my car. He couldn't be there and assault Annaleese at the same time.

*Unless...*I thought. *Unless they followed me together.*

If they'd carpooled to the Breakwater, the timing would have worked just about right, including my stop at the police station. Then it dawned on me that if Tanner followed me to Rockland, he most likely would have followed me back. He would have seen me talking with Sergeant Renvick in the police station parking lot. Maybe that's why he exploded on Annaleese. Perhaps if I'd gone into the police station like I had every other time, maybe he would have simply taken the bags from my backseat, and he wouldn't have gotten mad at all. Was this whole thing my fault? Certainly not! I chastised myself for thinking that way. I was probably the most innocent one entangled in this mess.

***

The evening dragged on. I sat in the chair, snuggled under a blanket the nurse had given me, and I waited for Annaleese to wake up. She'd been sleeping for hours. Visiting time had long since passed, but I was allowed to stay. As night drifted into dawn, sleep continued to elude me. I'd had more sleepless nights than I could count since Michael's death. As I sat and stared at my dead husband's mistress, I silently wondered what it was she loved so much about him. For all I knew, she'd simply performed a terrific show on the pier that day, screaming and crying like he was the love of her life. Was he? I wondered. Or was he part of the job, like I now was? Did she tease and taunt him, roping him into her money laundering world? Is that how Tanner got caught up in it all? Was he an innocent bystander until I called him that day? Who the hell was the guilty one here? I couldn't quite figure it out. Every time I found myself down a path that made sense, I'd remember something else that would demolish my rationale.

Suddenly, I heard a commotion in the hall, and I quickly moved to the side where I was out of sight of the glass door.

"Sir, you can't go in there!" A voice called out. "Sir! Sir!"

The glass door flung open and to my shock and disbelief, in walked Michael, my husband, very much alive. I watched as he all but ran to Annaleese's bedside. He reached out and gently took her hand, pressing his lips to her swollen ones. I watched in horror as he cried over her mangled body. Sobs shook him to the core, and then the room exploded with excitement as police officer after police officer filed through the door, wrestling him to the ground. They handcuffed him, the man who'd vowed the rest of his life to me, and as he was lifted to his feet, his eyes met mine. He didn't say a word; his mouth dropped open as they rushed him out of the room.

The police officers left, and the nurses rushed in to check on their patient. I sank to the floor in the corner, bewildered. Astonishment quickly escalated to total madness. A nurse knelt beside me. She placed her fingers on my wrist and reached for the air mask.

"I'm fine, I'm fine," I lied. "I need to get out of here. I... I can't stay. I can't stay."

I stumbled to my feet and was met at the door by the cops still on the other side.

"Can we help you?" They said in unison.

"Let me out of here!" I demanded through clenched teeth.

"We were told to guard you." The one on the right chirped.

"Then guard me as I walk away." I glared at him.

They looked at each other and shrugged. They looked to be fresh out of the academy. Young. I strutted past them and headed for the exit. As the glass doors opened to the outside world, another police officer stood in my way.

"Miss." He acknowledged me with a nod.

"I need to leave." I took a deep breath. "Listen, just radio Sergeant Renvick. He knows me."

"Who?" the veteran officer asked.

"Sergeant Todd Renvick," I explained slowly. "He's a detective here in town."

"Ma'am, I've been an officer of the law here for almost forty years. I've never heard of a Sergeant Renvick."

"Well, I think you should consider retiring because you are quite obviously losing your mind." I laughed, agitated. "He was here a little while ago. He's the one who ordered all this extra security." I waved my arm around the waiting room and adjacent hallway.

"I'm sorry, Ma'am." The officer remained firmly planted in the doorway.

"Hold on." I held one finger up between us and quickly spun around to the front desk. I grabbed the phone from the bewildered receptionist and dialed 911.

"Dirty green seal," I said to the operator.

"Excuse me?" came the reply.

"Dirty green seal," I spoke slower and louder. The entire waiting room looked at me like I was crazy.

"Ma'am? This is 911 emergency services. How may I help you?" The operator spoke deliberately.

"I need to speak with Sergeant Todd Renvick. He's a detective with the Camden police," I sighed.

"I'm sorry, Ma'am. We have no one by that name in our database."

I threw the phone across the room in an angry fit of rage.

"Ma'am, you need to calm down." The elderly officer attempted to strong-arm me.

I looked up at him with tears in my eyes.

"You really don't know him?" I whispered, pleading for him to say he remembered Vick.

"I'm sorry, Ma'am. We don't know a Sergeant Renvick."

I took my final breath and welcomed the end of my existence; certain I was dying from pure confusion. I felt my body go limp and the next thing I knew, I was waking up in a bed next to Annaleese.

My how the tide can change so quickly. The things we thought we knew, the things we were so sure of, can change in the blink of an eye. I awoke with a pounding headache. I wasn't in a hospital gown or hooked to machines. I was lying in my clothes. Did they think Annaleese and I were friends? I did transport her here and worry at her side for hours, but I certainly wouldn't classify us as friends.

Before I could stop it, my mind remembered the scene with Michael and the police officers. I sat straight up in the bed, my head loudly begging me to lay back down. Annaleese opened her eyes, her head tilted toward me. I opened my mouth to speak to her, even though I had no idea what to say, but the door opened before I could say a word. This was the day that just kept on giving, like waves beating repeatedly over the rocks, forging and molding them into something entirely different. My body tensed with irritation as Gerald Black stepped into the room.

"Thank you," he spoke to the police officer on guard, nodding as the young man closed the door. The click of the metal latch was deafening in my ears.

"Gerald?" I said, wildly confused. I squinted my eyes at his frame.

His dress shoes tapped loudly on the floor as they closed the gap between us. I opened my mouth to scream, not very impressed with our fine gentlemen in uniform. Gerald held up one finger as if the warning gesture would calm me down. Fat chance, not after the day I'd had!

"Listen to me." He spoke in a voice barely above a whisper. "Finally, both of you bitches in the same room. Quite honestly, I don't know what my son saw in either of you."

"He's not dead, Gerald." I blurted out the words.

Annaleese snapped her head in my direction as if the news shocked her. I rolled my eyes at her deer-in-the-headlights expression.

"Of course, he's not dead." Gerald raised himself onto his toes as he talked, adding to his stature in an effort to intimidate us.

"What?" Annaleese spoke for the first time since I'd picked her up off the side of the road. She didn't move her jaw much, but she spoke just the same.

"I've had enough of this shit show!" Gerald continued.

"But Sergeant Renvick said..." I started to argue.

"Todd Renvick is my associate." Gerald put his hands in his pockets. "As is Tanner Wilden, P.I. Now..."

"What?" I interrupted him. "What the fuck?"

"Now Macie, what did I tell you when you first showed up on my doorstep with my son?"

I didn't respond.

"I told you Michael knows what's expected of him. I told you that was not you. Correct?"

Again, I remained mute, silently wishing I could shoot fire out of my eyes like Clark Kent.

"Neither of you are good enough for Michael." He pointed both index fingers at us directly. "Is that clear, ladies?" He looked intently at Annaleese this time. She nodded her head obediently, cowering like a beaten dog.

"Wait a minute! Do you two know each other?" I finally found my voice.

"Of course we do, dear. I employ her." Gerald's voice was patronizing.

I looked at Annaleese with her swollen face and broken knee. One of her eyes could barely open but tears streamed from both.

"The card..." I whispered, mortified. "What exactly are you sorry for?"

"Ladies!" Gerald steered us back on track. "I encourage both of you to move on. Move elsewhere. Continue with your lives and forget about all of this." He stepped closer to Annaleese. "The mission is complete; you're paid in full. I'm sorry things got so messy."

With that, Gerald Black left.

I turned to look at Annaleese. I couldn't find any words other than 'I should have left you on the side of the street', so I didn't say anything. I simply went to her and patted her head slightly, almost feeling sorry for her, but not quite.

I walked out of the room, not looking back. I walked past the guards and out the front door. I walked in a daze to the nearest cafe and asked to use the telephone. I reached into my jacket pocket and pulled out a folded-up piece of paper, then I dialed the number on it.

"Hello?" Nadia's sweet voice brought unbidden tears to my eyes immediately. I sobbed into the receiver.

"Hello?" Nadia repeated herself.

"It's Macie." I managed between sobs.

"Macie, what's wrong?" Nadia's voice was laced with concern.

"Please come get me," I cried.

"I'm leaving now," she promised.

EIGHT

Have you ever wondered what it might be like to leave your life behind completely? To simply say 'enough of this' and start over somewhere new, somewhere fresh? To get a new job, a new apartment, a new identity? That's what I thought about the entire ride to New Hampshire with Nadia. Vince was out of town on business, so she'd come to my rescue alone. I didn't speak to her. I barely hugged her hello. I got in her front seat, locked the doors, and closed my eyes as we drove away. I couldn't speak. I didn't know how to decipher everything that had just happened. It was all chaos.

"Honey, are you okay?" Nadia patted my arm as she drove.

"I will be," I finally whispered. "Just get me out of here."

A tear escaped my eye, and I reached up to wipe it away before it could slide down my cheek. *No more tears*, I promised myself.

"Well, I'm glad you called. We've been wondering about you and how things are going." Nadia smiled. "I'm here to listen if you need to vent. Sometimes it's helpful to say things out loud while everything's fresh."

I looked out at the horizon as we whizzed down US Route 1. The sun was rising, we could see the sky changing colors in the rearview mirror. Nadia kept smiling at me and I struggled to recall a moment when she wasn't smiling. She was such a nice, genuine person. People like her were few and far between. For a brief second, it crossed my mind to kill her. I could stab her in the throat with a pen if we stopped to use a restroom between here and there. I could kill her and take her car. Maybe she was one of them, but I needed her too much to go down that road. The road of constantly looking over my shoulder. The road I'd been on for far too long already. I needed Nadia like I needed air to breathe. She could help me, and if she happened to be one of them, I didn't have much left to lose anyway.

"I'm going to take the scenic way home," Nadia said when I didn't speak. "There's an adorable little place in Bethel that does an amazing brunch on Sundays. It's a couple of hours from here, so you just sit back, relax, nap, take it easy. Alright?"

I nodded and I think I smiled. I couldn't feel my face move but I'm sure it did. I felt numb and unresponsive. Nadia turned the radio on low and I finally drifted off to sleep. When I awoke the sun was high in the sky, attempting to warm this late fall day. I was looking out the car window, trying to figure out my location, when I heard Nadia beside me in the driver's seat.

"Well, hello, sleepyhead!" She giggled at me.

"Hello." I yawned and stretched and smiled slightly. "Where are we?" I asked.

"We're in Bethel." She smiled.

I looked around at the almost bare trees and quaint townhouses. The brilliant blue sky seemed inviting, promising hope that was just out of reach but there, nonetheless. I breathed in deeply.

"Oh yes, brunch!" I remembered.

"Well, I guess they only do brunch in the summer. It makes sense, I suppose; they have a nice patio out front. They open for lunch in about ten minutes if you're hungry."

"Is it lunchtime already? Did I sleep that long?"

"You did." She nodded.

"I'm sorry," I apologized.

"Don't be! You needed to sleep. I caught up on some emails. Are you hungry?"

"I'm famished!" My stomach growled at the prospect of food. "But I have to be honest, I don't have any money," I admitted meekly as I remembered I didn't have my bag and even if I did, my only working credit card was Tanner's. My skin crawled at the thought of him.

"Honey, don't you worry about that!" She clutched my hand tightly in hers.

A few moments later, a line started forming outside the small cafe. Nadia and I followed suit, joining in with other excited patrons. The town seemed sleepy. I took a deep breath, inhaling the crisp air as if it could revive me from the outside in.

"I can't believe I slept so long," I whispered to Nadia. "You should have woken me!"

"You must have needed it!" She replied.

The door opened and we were greeted by a super friendly hostess. She told us to sit wherever we were comfortable, so I led the way to a corner table and sat facing the door. The place smelled of garlic and soy sauce and freshly baked bread, immediately reminding me of my very empty stomach. I couldn't remember the last time I ate. Breakfast yesterday, maybe? The decor was Asian, complete with a spectacular bamboo bar top that created a fun yet classy atmosphere.

"This place is delicious!" Nadia licked her lips. "Sometimes Vince and I will drive the two and a half hours just for lunch!"

I smiled back at her but didn't say anything as the server gave us menus and glass Ball jars full of cold water.

"You have to try a little bit of everything!" Nadia recommended as I gulped my water. The cold liquid felt reviving in my parched mouth.

"You order," I said between swallows.

The server returned and Nadia ordered us a pork Bahn mi, hot noodles, and an order of candied brussels.

"We have to save room for dessert!" She winked at me and handed our menus back to the server. "Oh, and can we get two pickle martinis? Also, we'd like fries with the meal too!"

I looked at her with respect. She'd definitely been here before. She knew what she was doing, right down to ordering extra aioli. I felt so comfortable with Nadia. She made me feel at ease. She didn't pry or poke me for details, even though I'm sure it was clear I was more of a mess now than I was a month ago if that even seems possible.

I don't know how she did it, but Nadia chattered away through the entire meal. She was right too; this place was superb. Handcrafted deliciousness in each aromatic bite: well worth the two-hour drive for lunch any day!

"What's this place called again?" I asked between bites of a crispy golden chewy roll loaded with flavorful pork, pickled veggies, and fresh cilantro. Every bite melted in my mouth, leaving me salivating for more.

"Le Mu," Nadia replied. "Isn't it great? And all of this started in a little food truck, or shanty as they called it. I love the beautiful artistic flare and the popping flavors! Mmm...so good!"

I smiled at her as she spoke and even dared to realize that her smile was rubbing off on me, causing mine to mirror hers more and more. I longed to forget everything else and focus solely on this ambrosial moment.

An hour later, our hunger satisfied, we hit the road again but not before Nadia ordered two rice bowls and two Angry Rooster chicken sandwiches that we would gladly devour for dinner later on. Bethel seemed peaceful, mellow even, like the calm before a storm.

"This place will be crazy busy in a few weeks," Nadia said. "Once Sunday River Ski Resort opens you can't even buy a tomato in this town."

That's how Camden was in the summer months, I thought, my mind instantly drifting back to the shallow sadness I'd been drowning in. I couldn't allow myself the gift of healing, not yet. I couldn't wrap my mind around what had happened in the last month. Longer than that, more like the last seven years. I still wore my wedding band. I'd tried to take it off several times, but the subtle action seemed impossible. The new widow in me wasn't prepared for my reality, and now, Michael wasn't dead at all. Now I fought the urge to toss the insignificant round band out the window as we drove west through the mountains. How was I supposed to process all of this? I couldn't. I simply couldn't.

In my moment of utter defeat, I looked at Nadia. Her portrait in the driver's seat was so serene. She was in control. I felt relief, sweet relief that I was no longer alone. A quiet confidence began brewing inside me, perhaps from the martinis at lunch.

"My husband isn't dead." I heard myself say the words as laughter bubbled up in my chest. "He's not dead and his father planned this whole thing to get rid of me." I chuckled.

"What?" Nadia said, mortified.

"Oh girl," I sighed and caught my breath. "I don't even know where to start."

"Are you serious?" she said, horrified.

"It's such a long story, and you're supposed to get your bail money back," I remembered that little detail as I spoke. "But I guess I don't know how because that asshole lied to me. Played me like a fucking fiddle!"

"We're not worried about that." She waved her hand in the air. "Tell me what happened. Start at the beginning."

"The beginning." I blew out a long breath. "Well, I guess the beginning would be when Michael first brought me home to meet his dad. Gerald told me I wasn't good enough for his son, in no uncertain terms. He didn't like me. I knew he didn't like me. He never hid the fact. I had no idea how deep his hatred went..."

"Sounds like a gem of a man." Nadia gripped the steering wheel tightly.

"After Michael's death, after you guys dropped me off at the police station, I moved in with Tanner." I paused for reaction.

"Your private investigator?"

"Yes, but there's more," I continued. "My arrest was fake. They said they wanted me to go undercover, to help find and prosecute Michael's killer, who they believed to be Tanner."

"What?" Nadia all but slammed on the brakes.

"They told me they knew Tanner killed Michael. There was DNA evidence on a missing boat or what have you," I summarized.

"Then why didn't they arrest him?" Nadia inquired.

"They told me he was a prime suspect in a money laundering expedition involving a yacht that docks in Camden Harbor on the first of every month. They wanted me to get close with Tanner in hopes of leading them to the base of the operation." I purposefully left out the part of me giving Tanner my divorce papers and not Michael. I felt stupid enough without adding that on top of it. "So anyway, I moved in with Tanner." I shivered at the recollection. "A little while after I moved in, I spotted Annaleese at Tanner's house getting a black duffle bag out of his shed, so I knew she was in on it too."

"The mistress?" Nadia asked for clarification.

"Yes." I nodded. "After that things were pretty stagnant for a while. I did the best I could, living with my husband's killer. Then Michael's mother called me yesterday, desperate to meet. I met her and she gave me five big black duffle bags full of cash. Full!"

"Really?" Nadia's mouth dropped open.

"Oh yes, you can't make this shit up!" I laughed. "So, of course, I went to the police station and told the detective I'd been working with."

"What did he say?" she asked.

"Not a lot. I told him I was going to give the bags to Tanner, that it would help gain his trust. On the way home, I spotted Annaleese walking on the side of the road. She'd been beaten. By Tanner. It was bad, I mean bad. So, I took her to the emergency room. I called the detective, and he met me at the hospital but while we were inside, someone stole my car and all the bags of money.

"What?" Nadia gasped.

"Hold on, hold on, it gets better," I warned her. "So, I'm there, in the room with Annaleese, waiting for her to wake up, and who do you think strolls in to be with her? To check on her, to cry over her bruised and battered body? Michael!"

"Your husband? Dead Michael?" Nadia pulled the car over and stared at me.

"Very much alive Michael," I nodded. "And to make matters worse, if possible, none of the policemen there knew who Sargeant Renvick was. Not one! Officers who'd been on the force for forty years had never heard of him! So, I had a little bit of a breakdown, passed out from sheer exasperation, and ended up in the same hospital room with Annaleese. That's when Michael's dad came in. He reminded me that he told me I wasn't good enough for his son, and that he always gets his way. Then he tells me that Renvick, Tanner, and Annaleese are all his associates. He told me to walk away and never return. That's when I called you."

"Macie..." Nadia was speechless as she held my hand in hers.

"It's just all so...so...patriarchal!" I stared out the windshield at the bare trees awaiting winter.

"It's all so illegal!" Nadia exclaimed. "And inhumane, and illegal!"

"Right?" I squeezed her hand. "Thank you so much for coming to get me."

"Oh, honey." Nadia had tears in her eyes.

"I just need to be away from it all for a bit. I need to regroup." I admitted.

"You are welcome to stay with us for as long as you need to," Nadia proclaimed.

"I don't have anything," I said.

"Don't you worry about a thing!" Nadia assured me, calming my lingering apprehensions.

"Do you think I should have stayed?" I looked deep into her eyes as I spoke the thought that wouldn't go away.

"Oh girl," she smiled softly. "I think there's only so many minutes in this life and we get to choose how we spend them. Besides, karma can be a way bigger bitch than prison ever thought of being."

I reached over and wrapped my arms around my newfound, forever-missing friend.

"We need to get out of here," Nadia sighed, "or else we're going to end up going back to Le Mu for more pickle martinis!"

NINE

Later that week, I sat on Vince and Nadia's glassed-in deck overlooking pristine Lake Winnipesaukee. It wasn't Camden Harbor, but it was just as beautiful in its own way. Camps, cottages, and exquisite mansions dotted the lake on all sides. This was nature's ultimate playground where, from Memorial Day to Labor Day, the lake was sprinkled with pontoon party boats, jet skis, and half-naked people. It wasn't the ocean, but my inner Pisces was soaking up every moment of this restful retreat.

"We're not broken, just bent." One of my favorite songs roared softly from the corner speaker, and I wondered how true that statement was. I surely felt broken. So many obnoxious questions floated in my brain, the most important of which was: If I went back home would I still be married? I never filed my copy of the divorce papers. I thought Michael was dead. It would have been ridiculous to prance into the courthouse and file divorce papers. Now what? If I knew Gerald well enough, I'm sure he'd figure out a way to legalize everything. The problem was I had no address, at least not one I wanted to share at this point. Could I forget about the last seven years? The last month? Yesterday? Was I broken or could I bend?

"Someone is deep in thought." Nadia entered the sunroom with two cups of tea. She had transformed me into a tea drinker this last week and I found it to be quite soothing, calming even. It was something I looked forward to each day.

"I wish I could stop thinking altogether," I sighed.

"I'm sure you do," Nadia replied.

"Can I ask you a question?" I eyed her carefully.

"Of course." She sipped her tea.

"You and Vince, no kids?" I'd been wandering about their gorgeous lakeside home for almost a week now and saw no evidence of children.

"No kids," Nadia said the words slowly.

"You didn't want kids?" I asked.

"No," she giggled. "Is that bad?"

"Oh, I don't know. I don't think so." I shrugged. "That's why I'm asking you."

"We decided we wanted a simple life. No kids, less restrictions and commitments."

I nodded. It sounded good, this life of Nadia's. It sounded like just what I needed.

"Not everyone has the same goals, you know?" Nadia smiled at me from behind her teacup.

"I just...I need a complete reset," I explained. "I don't know how to do that if I'm still married."

"Maybe you should get a post office box," Nadia suggested.

"I have email." I perked up, not knowing how I could have overlooked the ease of technology. "Do they send court documents via email?" The truth was, I didn't want a PO box. I didn't want anyone to know where I was. It presented a problem. I knew I couldn't live like this forever.

"I can't live my life in limbo," I sighed. I set my tea down and stood up to gaze out the impeccably clean window.

"These people sound dangerous." Nadia voiced the root of the problem.

"You know, the longer I think about it, the angrier I become. It's sickening. Disgusting, the things I did to help them. I feel so violated and dirty and no matter how many hot showers I take in your gorgeous bathroom, those feelings won't go away. It's haunting and that's in me. In here," I put my hand to my chest. "I can't hide from it; I can't run away. It's like I'm defective now."

Nadia stood up and joined me at the window. She rubbed my back but didn't say anything. What was there to say? What could possibly help?

Later that evening Vince arrived home from his work trip to Madrid. He worked in stocks. I didn't understand anything about the stock market other than it seemed to be lucrative for Vince. Nadia ran to greet him in the garage, presumably to update him on my mood. Vince and Nadia were sweethearts. It was a rare thing to see people so into each other. They were so invested in each other's lives. A few minutes later, Vince walked into the sunroom like a man on a mission and wrapped me in a massive bear hug.

"Hey there, 'bout time you got home!" I attempted to joke.

"Trust me, if I could have gotten here sooner, I would have." He pulled back from me. "I'm glad you're here," he said.

He was so sincere, so genuine. I don't know how I got to be so blessed to stumble into a life with Vince and Nadia. They were angels, both of them. Nadia brought in more hot tea and a cup for Vince. We sat there in the sunroom looking out over the glistening water willing the sun's energy to somehow fix the situation. If you're not broken, just bent as the song goes, how much time does it take for the bend to strengthen?

"We were just talking about living in limbo." Nadia broke the silence, catching Vince up to speed.

"Ah, limbo." Vince sipped his tea. "Well, you know how to get out of limbo?"

"I don't, actually," I chuckled at the thought.

"You need a plan. You're only in limbo if you don't have a plan." He took another sip of tea.

I sat back on the couch. Was that true? Was it that simple?

"I'm not at all undermining what you've been through," he continued. "It infuriates me beyond measure."

I watched as his face reddened and the veins in his forehead became more pronounced.

"Nadia and I are enraged that people behave the way they do. I'm so sorry this happened to you, Macie."

I took a deep breath, willing myself not to cry.

"Let us help you make a plan," he offered, holding Nadia's hand as he spoke.

"I don't... I don't know where to start or even what I want," I admitted meekly.

"Allow me to tell you our plan?" he suggested, his voice laced with temptation.

"Sure," I smiled at him.

"Well, as you know, we were in Camden looking for a place to retire to in a couple of years. We found a beautiful spot overlooking the ocean on Calderwood Lane. It's farmland, so peaceful, and right on the water. We have to be near water."

"Obviously," Nadia chirped in, waving her hand around at the sparkling lake.

"I'm going to say this, and you can do what you will with it," Vince continued. "I know we haven't known you very long and it's probably premature to say we *know* you at all, but from everything I've seen so far, you are scrappy. It's a good thing!" He insisted as Nadia's face grew into a mortified expression. "I'm saying you have a lot of grit, a lot of fight in you! You had the chance to run away when we were with you in Camden, and you didn't. You stayed. You're strong, Macie. Just because you're here now doesn't mean you're running away. May I suggest this: Stay here with us. Make a plan, find a job, and save some money. Allow yourself to heal and grow and then when we move to Camden, come with us. You don't have to stay away forever."

I let Vince's words rumble around in my mind for a minute. His perspective was fresh, just what I needed to hear. I couldn't go back right now. I had nothing to go back to. Part of my problem was I couldn't quite shake the feeling of defeat if I were to stay away. Now Vince was offering me a third option.

"What if I'm not welcome back there?" I voiced my obvious concern. Gerald had told me to leave, to start over elsewhere.

"A lot can change in two years. Hell, a lot can change in a day." Vince spoke wisely. "Karma can be a real bitch."

"That's exactly what Nadia said!" I laughed.

"It's true!" he defended his words.

"I hope so," I sipped my tea. "I struggle with the feelings associated with never going back." I confided in my new friends. "I feel run off, chased away even. And you're right, I'm not someone who backs away easily. I love it there; it's home."

"You have great instincts, Macie," Vince complimented me.

"Ha!" I almost spit my tea out. "Clearly, that's not the case!"

"You do!" he insisted. "Don't let these people make you think you don't. You knew when enough was enough. You knew when you'd reached your limit. You knew to come here. Now you can take this time to regroup, rejuvenate, and strengthen yourself. When we go back together, you can get divorced and resume living."

"Resume living..." I repeated his words. "I need to figure out what I want to do with my life."

"What interests you," Nadia asked.

"Truth be told, I was getting pretty into all the detective work." I shook my head as if to clear it.

"There's a community college right here. I think they have a criminal justice program!" Nadia squirmed in excitement.

"That's what you need to do." Vince nodded his head. "You take this anger and frustration, and you fuel yourself with it. You get them back, from the inside out."

I bit my bottom lip as a smile slowly spread across my face.

"Thank you," I said appreciatively. "Thank you both so much, more than you'll ever know."

Vince and Nadia were single-handedly saving me; picking me up off the ground, dusting me off, and arming me with the tools I needed to proceed. And proceed I would.

"Let's switch this tea to champagne, shall we?" Vince hopped up off the couch and hustled into the kitchen.

"I'm going to go help him get out of those dirty airplane clothes." Nadia winked at me.

"Take your time!" I giggled.

***

When the first day of school rolled around, I could barely contain my excitement. It was my first big step in reviving myself. I'd been too late to enroll in the fall semester, but Spring had finally arrived here in Laconia, bringing a newfound resolve. Nadia had also gotten me a job at her law firm. I mostly shuffled papers and ran errands, but it felt good to be working. It was ironic; this was my first real job after college, and here I was starting college all over again.

Life was good. I'd taken the winter to explore and develop my interests. I became obsessed with painting. In the Northeast, paint 'n sip nights are a popular winter activity. I went with Nadia to one on a quiet Tuesday evening, and I found it to be the most relaxing, fun thing I'd done in a while. It was at a local pub overlooking the tundra that was once Lake Winnipesaukee. It looked overwhelming at first, but stroke by stroke, my canvas evolved into a beautiful painting. I left feeling empowered, and I realized I needed more things in my life to make me feel this way.

Skiing was another thing I began doing for the first time in my now twenty-eight years. I went with Vince and Nadia one Saturday and was hooked immediately. It felt incredible to be doing things for myself, things I wanted to do, things that somehow made me feel more complete. The feeling became an addiction of its own.

Marriage is an easy thing to lose yourself in when you're young. It happens without you even realizing it. That's exactly how it had been with Michael and I. Things were always only about him, and before long, I'd become Mrs. Black, not Macie. Now, I was slowly but steadily building Macie back and it felt good.

Vince refused to let me help buy things. He wouldn't accept any money for rent or utilities. I think he felt as good helping me as I felt with each baby step in the right direction. I opened a bank account and started saving for my future. I hadn't heard a peep from my past life. Not one text, email, or phone call from Michael or anyone else. That's how I knew Gerald was still calling the shots, but I was too busy to worry about all that now. I was too busy becoming the person I wanted to be. I even went to the gym now. That was something I hadn't done since college the first time around.

Thankfully, my credits transferred from UMO to my new school here in Laconia and I was able to enroll in exciting classes right away rather than having to sit through college math or Intro to Lit. I signed up for one online class and one night class, figuring I'd start slow with my full-time job to boot. My night class, Principles and Practices of Investigation and Discovery, was on Wednesday nights at seven. On the first night, I wore my favorite new pantsuit. I felt like a boss when I walked into the classroom. My dress heels clicked along the floor as I walked. I took a seat in the lecture-hall-style classroom, in the center of one of the middle rows. I'd printed off the syllabus. I liked to have papers in front of me. I was a few minutes early, so I exchanged pleasantries with my neighbors, casually introducing ourselves and chatting about the weather.

"This professor is awesome," said a woman to my left. "I've had him for several courses. You'll love him!"

"What's his name?" I searched my syllabus for information.

"Matthew Walker," she replied without skipping a beat.

Just then, a man in a suit walked in carrying a briefcase and a Red Bull.

"Who drinks Red Bull at seven PM?" The woman to my right scoffed.

I barely heard her. All of a sudden, I had to focus on my breathing. My heartbeat sounded in my ears and I willed myself to stay calm.

"He does," I whispered incoherently. "He drinks Red Bull all the time."

It was true. Tanner Wilden drank Red Bull like it was going to disappear. As a PI and an associate to a money launderer, I suppose he had to stay alert.

"Hello everyone." Tanner's voice made me want to vomit. "Professor Walker sends his deepest apologies, but he won't be teaching this semester. I am Tanner Wilden. I own and operate a private investigation firm. Your first assignment in this class is going to be to go out there in this big scary world and watch what you perceive to be a real crime. I want a five-page paper next class on what you watched take place, where it was, and why you think it was a crime. How much do our personal perceptions play into what we think we see? What triggers your instincts, if anything, and what determines the difference between the guilty and the innocent? That's it. Thank you. See you next week."

I sat immobile in my seat, unable to move until the crowd around me began to disperse. I thought of leaving also, of shuffling out with everyone else, but the pangs of panic bubbling up inside my chest didn't scare me, they infuriated me. I watched Tanner shake hands with students as they exited the bottom doorway. I stood and walked down the stairs toward him. When the last student left, he turned to me with both hands stuffed into his pockets.

"Mrs. Black." He bowed his head toward me. "You're not a very hard person to find."

"That's because I'm not hiding," I said cooly.

Tanner didn't respond. He eyed me up and down, and at that moment, I wondered if he was mad at me too. After all, I'd been working undercover to ruin him. That had been my only goal, while his was to do the same to me. We'd used each other, in that regard. Playing off each other, deceiving each other. The only difference was, he'd known the plan from the start. I had not.

"What are you doing here?" I asked sharply, my voice echoing in the empty room.

"I'm teaching Principles and Practices of..."

I slapped him hard, square across his jaw.

"Don't fuck with me!" I seethed. "What are you doing here?"

"Macie. Macie, I miss you. I know... I know I shouldn't say that but it's true, I do." He rubbed his jaw tenderly.

"Go to Hell!" I glared into his eyes before brushing past him and bursting through the double doors.

***

"Maybe it's time we go to the police," Vince said later that night.

"He must have found my name in a database when I enrolled in classes. This is not a coincidence. He doesn't teach college. He was searching for me. Plus, I mean, like I told him, I'm not hiding. I get actual paychecks. I'm using your address. Oh my God! Guys! I'm using your address!" My hands flew to my mouth. The last thing I wanted was to endanger Vince and Nadia any more than I already had.

"It's fine." Nadia laid her hands on top of mine as we sat at their kitchen table.

"I'll start looking for my own place tomorrow," I insisted.

"You will do no such thing." Vince wouldn't hear it. "You will stay right here."

"Let's have him over for dinner!" Nadia shocked Vince and me with her suggestion. We both stared at her blankly. "What?" she continued. "It would be intimidating for him, I would assume, to be openly invited here. It would set the tone, and the tone being that you are not alone, you are not scared, and you are in control."

"I like it." I nodded slowly as my mind comprehended her twisted plan. "Like I told him, I'm not hiding. I'll ask him next week if you're sure."

"I make no promises of compatibility," Vince said holding both hands up in the air.

"Yes, let's do it!" Nadia said persistently.

I chuckled and shook my head, acknowledging the insanity of it all. Then I poured us more wine.

TEN

As the week progressed, I struggled to maintain initiative. Regardless of who the professor was, I knew I had to complete the assignment. Not only did I have to complete it, I had to excel at it. I didn't want any favors. My work had to be excellent on all fronts.

Watch what you perceive to be a crime... Where should I go to study people, I wondered. Then it hit me that I didn't even need to leave the couch. I could write about what was unfolding right in front of everyone. A criminal impersonating a professor with the sole purpose of ultimate manipulation, betrayal an unforeseen hazard. I sat down at the small table overlooking Lake Winnipesaukee, and I opened my laptop.

> *"A thief and a murderer walk through the freshly fallen snow; one set of footprints making their way to the academic complex. He enters the classroom and introduces himself as the instructor for the semester. Unbeknownst to everyone else, the impersonator is an imposter; his crimes are too many to numerate. What motivates someone of this caliber? What guides their decision-making? I dare say, greed. Greed and loneliness..."*

My fingers typed steadily, barely able to keep up with my thoughts. The trickiest part of investigative work was always determining motivation. Motivation is what makes a criminal a criminal. Deconstructing guilt and innocence was easy once motive was determined. I was learning this in my online course.

I reread my five-and-a-half-page paper and hit the submit button on my screen. *There.* I thought to myself. *Take that, Professor Wilden.*

When I got up the next morning, I rushed to check my email, half expecting a rebuttal from Tanner. There was none. I refreshed the page. Still nothing. I showered and dressed for work, convincing myself he hadn't read it yet. It was a larger class than I'd anticipated, perhaps he was swamped with papers.

Over the weekend, still no reply. I double-checked and triple-checked to make sure I'd hit send. I had, and it appeared to have been received. I'd have to wait until class for a response. Tuesday crawled by. Work was monotonous, a steady stream of menial tasks that failed to get my mind off Tanner. I wondered if inviting him to dinner would be too abrasive. I wore my favorite charcoal gray pencil skirt with black high heels. I'd recently discovered height made me feel brave, and as I finally walked to the lecture hall that evening, I needed all the bravery I could muster.

"Ms. Black," Tanner greeted me like he did all the other students.

I paused and looked him deep in the eyes. "It's Mrs." I clarified briskly and kept walking.

"I trust you all had a good week," Professor Wilden started. "I must say, I enjoyed reading your papers. If you haven't passed yours in yet, allow me to remind you it was due today. You're late."

He seemed to be looking directly at me and for a moment I wondered if I attached my paper correctly. Then, to my horror, he turned on the overhead projector and my paper lit up for everyone to see.

"I'd like to discuss this one, in particular, as it caught my attention immediately. You'll see why." He began to read my amateur investigative report out loud. Students on both sides of me whispered.

"Let's discuss, shall we?" Tanner sat on the edge of the big metal block desk. "Let's talk about motivation. Ms. Williams, what's your motivation for taking this course?"

A tall, slim woman two seats to my left stirred in her seat before answering.

"I need the credit to complete my degree," she replied honestly.

"So, would you say duty motivates you?" Tanner asked.

"Yes," she responded.

"What about you, Ms. Lockely?"

"I'm a psych major." The woman directly to my left answered. "I thought this class sounded interesting."

"You're motivated by intrigue?" Tanner deducted, nodding his head. "And you, Ms. Aimsly? What motivated you to take this class?"

"I'm a single mom. This class fits my busy schedule." The slightly plump brunette to my right answered shyly.

"Time could be your motivation then?"

"Yes sir," she replied, her face red.

"The author of this paper suggests greed and loneliness are the perpetrator's motives. Can anyone suggest a different motive?"

I waited, ready for him to call on me. I knew he'd skipped me on purpose in his line of questioning. He was always such an intimidator.

"Let's keep in mind that the assignment was to write a *perceived* situation. This is hypothetical," he chuckled, and the entire class chuckled too. Everyone, except me.

"What about guilt?" a young man behind me piped up. His thoughts about motivation were not lost on me, but Tanner Wilden was incapable of feeling guilt. How could he, after everything he'd done?

"Ah, yes! Guilt." Tanner hopped off the desk and strolled up the steps to where the male student was seated. "Guilt about what?"

"Guilt about his past choices, his crimes," the student explained.

"And why would a murderer and a thief choose to teach a class in a local university such as this one? This is a small community. Why would a criminal be so blasé as to risk being seen or caught?"

"Maybe he's trying to balance out his karma," the student replied.

"Ah, karma." Tanner nodded again and walked slowly back down the wide steps. "Any other thoughts?" he asked. The room remained quiet, so he continued. "I could ask each and every one of you what motivates you and could quite possibly receive a different answer each time. What motivates us is a personal thing. It's a unique experience for each of us. However, there is one motivator that is perhaps the most powerful of all. Any guesses?"

He walked to the whiteboard on the wall behind his desk and wrote one four-letter word in bold black marker.

LOVE.

I swallowed hard, my mouth suddenly very dry.

"Love." Tanner tapped the whiteboard with the tip of his marker, creating unnecessary dots on the white surface. "Love is one of, if not the strongest motivator there is. Love is at the core of most wars, after all. Love, and religion, but that's a different course entirely. For next week, I want you to presume your criminal is acting out of love. Why is he acting out of love? What do you think he hopes to accomplish by committing his crime? Should he get a lighter sentence if his motivation is love? I want your three-page papers on this mushy topic by Monday night and, just to be clear, I don't read late submissions. Have a good week."

With that, Tanner grabbed his briefcase and left the room, leaving all of us rather stunned and wondering if this two-hour course would ever go past twenty minutes.

Love. Are you kidding me? I bet it didn't feel like love when he was beating the crap out of Annaleese. Maybe he didn't love her...

I rationalized with myself as I sat alone in a crowded bar after class. This was a perk of being an older student. I could legally drink which worked out lovely this evening when coffee would just not do. It was my first time at this bar. It was the closest bar to campus, but I always passed by the bars in my desire to get home. Vince and Nadia were nothing short of amazing hosts and I preferred spending time with them over strangers in a bar. Tonight, I was mad. Beyond mad. How could Professor Wilden dare to insinuate such hypocrisy? Did he even know what love is? Did he love me? He'd never hurt me. On the contrary, he was quite gentle and well, loving even. I shuddered, quivering at the thought.

"Ma'am," the bartender placed a fresh Cosmopolitan in front of me. "Compliments of the man across the bar."

I looked up from the sleek pink drink to the bartender and followed his gaze directly to Tanner.

"Actually, I'll settle up with you if you don't mind." I pressed my credit card into the man's hand.

He took it, nodded, and rang up my drinks. When I looked back over to where Tanner had been, he was gone. I quickly signed the receipt and scanned the room again. I couldn't see him anywhere, so I settled back down in my seat and drank my charity beverage slowly. I didn't want to leave for fear that he was lingering outside waiting for me.

"Would you like me to give him a message?" The bartender was too helpful. Did he think his job was matchmaking?

"Who?" I said, confused. My senses suddenly felt dull, dazed.

"The man who bought you the drink." He smiled at me.

"Is he still here?" I ducked lower on the barstool.

"Yes, he moved to the corner table. Over there..." He started to point.

"Shhh!" I hissed as panic engulfed me.

"Ma'am? Ma'am, are you okay?" The bartender was concerned now.

I felt myself drift away. I could see myself; I watched the whole thing unfold. I slowly started leaning, falling over, and I heard a man's voice saying I was fine. He'd take care of me. I heard Tanner thank the bartender, assuring him I'd be fine. I felt myself stand up and then he lifted me into his arms, and I was gone, the bar doors swinging in the wind as we exited into the freshly fallen Spring snow.

***

I awoke to Nadia's whispering voice. She was irritated. I knew I should be on my way; I should stop being a burden to these nice innocent humans. Then I heard another voice and another, and I felt the world begin to spin. I kept my eyes tightly shut and my body still as I listened to Vince and Nadia arguing with Tanner. They were arguing about money, I gathered. Money really is the root of all evil.

"He's very late paying us!" Nadia spat.

"Listen," Vince cut in. "This has been a lucrative venture for us, as I'm sure it has been for you, we're just wondering what the end game is."

"The end game is none of your concern after tonight." Tanner's voice sounded threatening to me, but I wasn't sure if I'd ever heard him be any other way.

I peeked my eyes open a slit or two, just in time to see Tanner hand Vince and Nadia each an envelope. I closed my eyes again and silently vowed to disappear into the mattress. They were all working together! I never in a million years would have guessed that to be true. I should have. They'd shown up the day of the hurricane and conveniently bonded with me. It never crossed my mind they were too good to be true. How could I be so naive? I deserved to be lying here, dazed but unfortunately alert. I wished this were a dream. I begged the universe to let this be a dream, but when I opened my eyes again, Nadia noticed and was at my side in an instant.

"Fuck off!" The words slipped out of my dry lips before I could stop them.

"What? Macie..." She looked heartbroken. Vince appeared in a flash, and I searched the room for Tanner, but he seemed to have disappeared into thin air.

"Welcome back." Vince held my hand reassuringly. I quickly swiped it away from him.

"Macie, what's wrong?" Nadia looked genuinely concerned.

"Who are you?" I said to her, my eyes wild.

"What?" she repeated, taking a step back.

"Who are you?" I turned to Vince this time.

I watched as husband and wife exchanged a questioning glance.

"Where am I?" I decided playing dumb might be my best bet. I silently wished I'd skipped college classes altogether and got a job and my own apartment. Again, I found myself in the same boat as before, a half-rotten dingy with nothing but despair and broken dreams on the faded horizon.

Again, I had nothing of my own, no home, no family, clearly no friends or anyone without an agenda. What the hell was I supposed to do now?

Suddenly, without a care in the world, I tossed the blanket off myself and stood up. I was still dressed in the same clothes I had on the night before. It was barely light outside now. Dawn mimicked dusk and I had to check my watch for the time. It was barely six AM.

"Where is he?" I glared at my captors, unable to pretend any longer.

"Who?" Nadia and Vince said in unison.

"Don't fuck with me!" I warned them. "I heard you talking to Tanner."

"Macie, you must have been dreaming!" They both looked at me with concern painted all over their lying faces.

"I have to get out of here." I slid my boots on and without even stopping to gather my things, I walked out into the crisp morning air.

"Macie, Macie please, wait..." Vince followed me down the front steps and into the driveway.

"Don't follow me!" I spun around and yelled at him.

"Macie, please! You don't understand!" he called after me.

"Enlighten me then!" I stopped walking and stood face-to-face with him. Nadia watched from the kitchen window.

"We were paid to keep you safe, that's all," he explained, his hands moving frantically as he spoke.

"Paid by who?" I asked through gritted teeth.

"By him. By Tanner," he admitted reluctantly.

"How could you? I trusted you!" I stomped my foot on the icy, snow-covered driveway.

The thing about ice is, it's slippery. One would think I'd be aware of this since I'd lived in the Northeast my entire life. I watched my view change from Vince's face to the gray cloudy sky above us. I felt cold tar under my head and then warmth. My eyes closed and a faint ringing took up residence in my brain. Then all was dark.

ELEVEN

When I awoke, I was back in Tanner's bedroom in Belfast. I stretched and sat up in his big California king bed. The little white shed stared at me from outside the window. I wondered how many black duffle bags were in it now. How long had it been since I'd seen Annaleese walking out of it? A few months, not long at all. Tanner had all but imprisoned me here before, as he worked for my husband's father, but none of that seemed to matter now. He was as sly and untrustworthy as they come. I heard footsteps in the hallway outside the closed door and flattened myself again in the bed.

The door creaked open, singing a coarse tune of displeasure as it went. I kept my eyes closed. My head ached and my mouth was drier than I'd ever felt it before. I heard him breathing at the foot of the bed. Then I felt his hands slowly make their way up my body; the quilt and sheet between my skin and his were not nearly thick enough. I remained quiet. I was surprised and grateful he wasn't under the blankets.

Tanner's hands escalated from my legs and hips to my stomach and breasts, then my neck. He lingered at my neck, squeezing my throat ever so slightly. I played dead, part of me wishing that was the case, but most of me wanting to jump on him, to scare him, to take charge. Could I do that? Could I grasp his scrawny neck with both of my hands and strangle the life out of him? He was stronger than me, but I was angry. High voltage adrenaline pumped through my body. Surely, he could feel it in my veins that were now pulsating beneath his revolting touch. I was about to open my eyes and let fate determine my next move when he leaned down and kissed my cheek softly.

"I have something for you when you wake up," he whispered in my ear.

His mouth felt warm and wet in my hair. I kept my eyes shut, longing to be anywhere but here. He climbed off the bed, and I heard his shoes hit the floor.

Fuck this, I thought as he started to walk away. *I'm not waiting to see what he wants.*

"Tanner?" I sat up slowly as if I'd just woken from sedation. I held my head in my hands and rubbed both temples gingerly. Perhaps I had just woken from sedation. Did the asshole drug me twice? He must have.

"Macie, baby..." He was back at my side in an instant.

"Don't call me that." I glared at him.

He stopped short of sitting down on the bed and stood awkwardly at the edge.

"What's going on, Tanner? Fuck..." I let my voice drift off.

"I have something for you." He handed me a manila folder. His temperament was suddenly that of a fourth grader handing his mom a bad report card.

"What is it?" I asked skeptically.

He pressed it closer to me without saying a word.

"Tanner, for fuck's sake!" I swore between gritted teeth. "You won, alright. Obviously. You followed me to Laconia, you pretended to be a professor... Oh wait, back up, that's right! You plotted and planned this entire twisted escapade! Not that I expect you to tell the truth now...but why?"

He opened the manila envelope and laid two crisp papers on the quilt in front of me.

'CERTIFICATE OF DEATH', they both said at the top in big bold print. The first one read, GERALD BLACK, and the other, MICHAEL BLACK. I felt my jaw drop.

"Is this verifiable?" I asked, my voice barely above a whisper.

"Aren't you going to ask me how?" He seemed offended.

"No," I grunted. "I don't care how."

"He was your husband." Tanner was almost astonished at my abrasiveness.

"So?" The entire conversation irritated me. Everything about Tanner Wilden pissed me off.

"What about this warrants you drugging me? Following me?"

"This makes you a widow," he explained.

"Do I win a prize or something?" I rolled my eyes.

"You're free!" Tanner threw his arms up in the air.

I stared at him. The skin along my brow wrinkled as a dark scowl fell over my face.

"Do I look free to you?" I growled. I reached down and snatched the papers off the bed. I crushed them into little wrinkled balls and threw them at the man pretending to be my rescuer.

"I killed them for you," Tanner admitted. It seemed unfathomable to him that I wasn't grateful.

"Don't tell me that!" I shook my head.

"I did," he continued. "I killed them for us. We can be together now!"

"What about Annaleese? What about Vince and Nadia?"

"They are of no concern anymore. They are all paid in full."

"Why were they involved at all?" I asked.

"I needed to know you were safe." He swallowed hard, his Adam's apple rising and falling in his throat.

"Safe?" I laughed.

"I am not the bad guy here, Macie," he defended himself. I watched as his face slowly turned to crimson.

"You beat the shit out of Annaleese," I reminded him. "You've been laundering money out of your shed. You've been lying to me for months, years even! You were an asshole in elementary school. What kind of person is an asshole in third grade?"

Tanner looked down at the floor like a scolded dog. When he didn't say a word, I demanded he look at me, sounding much more confident than I felt.

"That was all my job," he insisted.

"You were employed in third grade?" I chuckled, unable to hide my irritation.

"Look, I don't have any excuses!" He threw his hands up into the air. "Yes, I've always been a dick. I've always done anything I could for money. Most of the time, I should have said no, I should have walked away. I should have been a better person. Do I regret hurting Annaleese? Of course, I do! I'm not the monster you think I am."

"No, you're worse," I whispered.

"Fine, leave." He backed up and motioned to the bedroom door.

I threw the covers off of me, my nakedness irrelevant, and slowly stood up. Dizziness cloaked me, and as hard as I tried, I could not help but sit back down.

"What can I do?" He was next to me in the blink of an eye.

"You already did this," I cried, hot tears spilling from my eyes.

"Baby, I'm so sorry." He pulled my body into his and caressed my soft skin as I cried.

I shook with sobs as my life unraveled in front of me. His hands moved slowly at first, from my hair and face down my neck to my naked breasts and stomach. He laid me down, ignoring my tears as he climbed on top of me. As much as I hated him, I was thankful for the distraction as his body slid into mine. I let him fuck me, knowing I didn't have any other options.

"I love you, Macie," he spoke into my ear between thrusts. "I love you enough to always find you."

I knew this would be my foreseeable future. What other choice did I have?

***

I've thought about murder many times, to say I haven't would be a gross understatement. I should have gone into Psychology. The human mind is just…it's intrinsically magical. Yes, I've thought of murder… somehow, somewhere, someone… I can't be the only one who thinks of these things. I've prided myself on living a life free of things like murder. Free of felonies and even misdemeanors. Now, as Tanner helped me shower for the fifth time in two days, I plotted his demise. Maybe he'd slip on a shower tile. Perhaps he'd strangle himself with the bedsheets in the middle of the night. Lord knows, all sorts of things can happen in the middle of the night.

My favorite thing to think about was poison. I didn't care that it was commonly known as a woman's weapon. I was a woman, and it would get the job done. I longed to look into Tanner's eyes after he sipped the last of his poisoned drink and watch as the life slowly drained from his twitching body. I'd watch with wonder. Wonder and satisfaction as blood streamed from his nostrils and lips. Ah, sweet satisfaction.

I'd never felt so trapped in all my life. It left me feeling nauseous and utterly defeated. Finally, at the start of my second week with Tanner, I decided to take matters into my own hands.

"I want to finish school," I said one night over dinner.

"Criminal justice classes?" he replied without looking up from his meal.

"Yes, it's the only thing that interests me," I smiled shyly.

"You don't have a mind for criminal justice," he said, his voice snarky.

"You don't know anything about my mind." I laid my fork down and sat back in my chair. "Furthermore, I think I hit the nail on the head in that class. Don't you?"

"Macie..." he sighed, stopping himself.

"What kind of life do you want here, Tanner?" I asked, frustrated. "Because I'm not the type of girl who is going to sit at home and bake pies and casseroles and knit blankets. I need a job. I need an outlet outside of here."

"You don't need a job," he argued. "We have plenty of money."

"You have plenty of money! I have nothing," I corrected him.

He sat forward in his chair across from me and rubbed his temples as if he were getting a migraine.

"Tanner," I continued. "I've tried to be okay with this, but I've been walking around here like a zombie for the last week. I need more than this in my life. I need purpose. I want to go back to school."

"That's impossible," he grunted.

"Why?" I pressed him even though I knew he was getting angry. "I'll do online classes."

"No," he glared at me.

"So, I'm just going to be trapped here forever?" I concluded.

"You're not trapped here." He threw his napkin on the table. "All I want is for you to want to be here."

"But I don't want to be here," I enunciated each word forcefully.

"Listen, we'll get married. We'll have a slew of kids. Then you'll have a purpose." He smiled at me before taking another bite of salad.

How would I even get poison? I wondered.

***

I'd never considered suicide until the night I felt my baby flutter in my belly. I'd been Tanner's prisoner for three months. Every day I was alert, constantly on guard, waiting to grasp onto anything that resembled survival. But survival never came. I had no friends. No outlets of any kind. While I wasn't locked up per se, I had no means of outside communication and no money. Tanner had taken my phone, and I wasn't allowed computer privileges. I did live quite comfortably with Tanner. He had expensive taste and, in turn, nice things. He never worked because he didn't trust me, yet he always had money. His ventures with the Blacks must have been very profitable. He didn't seem to have a care in the world. A happy life with Tanner would have come easily if I could allow myself the freedom of surrender, but I could not. I would not. I never rested. Freedom wasn't even a speck on the horizon.

As I stood at the kitchen sink watching the water disappear down the drain, I felt the baby tumble in my womb and I jumped, dropping a lone glass into the ceramic sink. It shattered and my blood began to drip onto the wet white surface. It pooled in the center of the sink, its color dulling to a soft pink before it too disappeared down the drain.

"Macie? Baby, are you alright?" Tanner was at my side in a flash and for a brief second, I thought of slitting my wrists with the jagged edge of the broken glass that rested in the bottom of the sink. After all, I couldn't raise a child in this mess. What would her life be like? I couldn't imagine. Suicide had never been an option for me. I never even considered it to be a last resort. I wouldn't give up. Now, as I stood staring into the sink, I knew there was another choice. My aim would have to be flawless.

"I'm fine," I said calmly. "I tripped on that spot on the floor."

His gaze followed my bloody finger to the floor by his right foot. He knelt to inspect whatever could have caused me to lose my balance. It's beautiful how adrenaline kicks in right when we need it to. I reached into the sink and pulled out the broken glass. I felt it slice my right hand as I gripped it and plunged it deep into the side of Tanner's neck. He fell forward, pulling at the shard of glass that protruded from his skin. My aim had been flawless, just as I knew it would be. I stepped back as he sprawled out on the floor, blood spilling from his flesh. It was a big chunk of glass. The thick beer mug had been one of two in his cupboard. An hour ago, when I set the table for dinner, I had no idea this glass would save my life. Save my child's life. I sat down at the table and watched Tanner expire. His twitching stopped, his body became still, and I knew for the first time that I would be okay.

"Jail would be better than being here with you," I whispered to his lifeless shell before picking up his phone and calling 911.

I sat numbly in the chair as the police arrived. They questioned me, some of the same faces as my night at the hospital with Annaleese. Did they believe me now? Did I have their attention now that I'd become a murderer? The EMT's checked me over. They bandaged my hand and gave me a light sedative, assuring me it wouldn't harm the baby. The baby that would now be fatherless. The baby that now might have a chance at survival.

The police told me not to leave town, but they didn't arrest me. I watched as the coroner zipped Tanner's body bag shut.

"What's the name of the college? Miss? Miss?" The detective shook me to attention.

"Laconia Community College," I blinked rapidly.

They would verify my story and be in touch. Did I have anywhere to stay tonight? Any family in the area? Friends? I shook my head at each question. I didn't have any friends or family or anywhere to go. I had nothing.

"I can take you to the Belfast Women's Center if you'd like. It's a shelter downtown." The man had kind eyes as he spoke.

"Can I stay here tonight?" I pleaded. "I'll figure out my next move in the morning."

"I don't see why not," the officer smiled. "We'll have an extra patrol in the area tonight. If you need anything at all, please don't hesitate to call." He handed me his business card, tipped his hat, and followed the coroner out the door.

I stood, got the mop out of the closet, and began sopping up Tanner's blood. I cleaned the floor until it couldn't shine any brighter. Then I went upstairs and packed a bag. I lined the bottom of the black duffel bag with bundles of cash, then clothes. I filled two bags this way. Tanner hadn't been stingy with my needs. He provided me with a brand-new wardrobe when he kidnapped me from New Hampshire. I took enough things to be comfortable. When dawn approached, I called the phone number on the police officer's business card and told him I wasn't fleeing, but I wanted to relocate to Camden. I couldn't stay in the house of the man I'd just murdered.

"No problem, Mrs. Black, you're all cleared anyhow. We've verified your identity and story. We're very sorry for all you've been through."

"Thank you," I stuttered into the receiver.

Then I called a cab and left Belfast without looking back. But not before going through Tanner's house and taking all the cash I could find. After all, I deserved it.

Murder had come easy to me. When you have nothing else to lose little chances seem like giant leaps. To anyone else, it would have appeared as though I'd saved my baby's life, but in reality, it was the other way around. The flutter I'd felt had jumpstarted my very existence. It wasn't just me anymore. Once that glass broke, adrenaline had taken over every ounce of my being and now I was free. Three split seconds had altered my life forever.

TWELVE

"You know he loved you more than anything else in this world?" Mrs. Wilden, Tanner's mother, cornered me in the grocery store a week later.

"Excuse me?" I backed away from the angry woman and almost bumped into a display of marshmallows and chocolate bars.

"You're her. You're Macie. I know," she said. She stood with one hand on her hip.

"How do you know?" I felt violated. Story of my life...

"He always showed me pictures of you." Her eyes softened enough so tears threatened to spill out. "I know he was troubled. He'd always been troubled." She sniffed.

"What do you mean by 'troubled'?" I asked slowly.

"He had an obsessive soul." She took a deep breath. "Especially with you. I should have warned you, I know. As his mother, I should have said something. He just... he was always so happy talking about you. I was happy because he was happy."

I nodded slowly and continued my way down the canned goods aisle of the supermarket. If she was expecting forgiveness, she'd be waiting forever. I rolled my half-full cart over to a sales associate and apologized before rushing out of the glass double doors.

"Fuck!" I screamed and banged my hands against my steering wheel. All I wanted was a life under the radar, where people would leave me alone. Everywhere I went someone approached me. A police officer reaching out to check on me, forgotten friends from my days with Michael, a past life it seemed now. Everyone was sorry. Everyone was concerned. Everyone was dying to help me in any way they could. All I wanted was to be alone; it was my deepest desire.

Later that evening, I lay curled in a ball on the bathroom floor, knowing with certainty that I was indeed alone now. In the wee morning hours, I dragged myself into the shower and let the water flow over my body.

"What a strange journey it's been," I whispered into the steam.

The next morning, I dressed in silence and convinced myself to go to the hospital. I grabbed my keys from the nightstand and opened my hotel room door. I'd been staying in Camden, across the street from the park, until I could determine what to do next. To my surprise, Annaleese stood on the other side of my door, her hand raised to knock.

"Annaleese," I whispered, startled.

"Macie." She smiled meekly at me.

"What are you doing here?" I struggled for words.

"I heard about Tanner," she swallowed hard. "I had to come check on you."

"Funny, no one came to check on me when he was alive," I sneered.

"Macie, I couldn't," she started to explain.

"You know what? It's fine," I held my hands up to quiet her. "I'm fine. Everything is fine." I brushed past her, slamming the door shut behind me. My stomach throbbed. I could feel sweat beading up on my forehead.

"It's not fine, Macie," she continued as she followed me down the interior corridor. "The way we treated you was so wrong..."

"Listen, I have to go. I'm in the middle of having a miscarriage." I fumbled for my keys and cried out loud when they fell to the floor.

"What? Macie, here, let me help!" She retrieved my keys and linked her arm in mine to assist me down the stairs.

A few minutes later we were pulling up to the emergency room doors.

"Don't leave your keys in the car," I advised her. "Just drop me off, I'm fine."

"I'm not dropping you off." She rolled her eyes at me. "Hold on, there's a parking spot right there."

She quickly parked and ran to get me a wheelchair.

"Thank you." I touched her arm. "I'm okay alone, honest."

Annaleese knelt next to the wheelchair and looked me directly in the eyes.

"You are not alone, and you'll never be alone again." She squeezed my hand, and I came dangerously close to allowing myself to feel something I hadn't felt in a very long time – comfort. I didn't say anything. I sat back and let her push me into the hospital. She never left my side, she held my hand the entire time, and when we left, she drove me back to my hotel and helped me pack my belongings.

"You can stay with me," she'd said, and I found I didn't have any strength left to argue.

***

Annaleese had a beautiful cottage on the shore. It was well-manicured and tucked away on a dead-end street. It screamed of dirty money, but I couldn't talk because so did my new car. I figured I'd earned every penny, and looking around at Annaleese's immaculate home, I was sure she'd earned hers too.

"I have to tell you something before you get too settled." She sat down on her big leather couch and motioned for me to do the same.

I walked over and sat beside her.

"It's important to me that you know how sorry I am for my role in everything that happened." She reached for my hand. "I'm very sorry, Macie, for everything. I thought I loved Michael. I thought he loved me..." She paused and wiped at her eyes. "It doesn't matter now anyway, but I'm sorry."

"It's okay, Annaleese," I rubbed her shoulder. "I'm sorry too, I know you must miss him."

"Miss him?" she looked at me with furrowed eyebrows.

"Well, I heard..." I started but she interrupted me.

"We broke up on mutual terms. It was for the best," she smiled fondly.

"But I thought..."

Suddenly the doorbell rang, interrupting me yet again.

"He loves you, Macie." She grinned at me like a twelve-year-old girl with a big secret.

"Who?" I asked, but Annaleese was already opening the door. Michael stared at me from the other side. My Michael. My supposedly dead husband.

Before I knew what I was doing, I was running to him, and he swept me up in his arms. Annaleese excused herself and Michael helped me to the couch where we talked for hours. He said how sorry he was for his many indiscretions. It all seemed so tiny now, a small slip of our vows. The thing that had turned my world upside down now felt like nothing more than a mistake.

"I thought you were dead, twice..." I heard my voice break halfway through my sentence.

"I'm not dead," he assured me.

"I'm not sure I'm alive," I whispered.

Then his lips were on mine as he breathed life back into my trembling frame of a body; the shell of a human I'd become. I let him kiss me. I let him hold me in his arms and I let myself relax until all of a sudden, the memories of the past year floated to the top of the waters within me. Images of him with Annaleese, images of what I thought was his dead body bopping around in the angry ocean waters, images of freshly printed money and Seargant Renvick's fake leg. Flashbacks of Tanner's body on top of mine, his hands around my neck, his body throbbing inside mine, frightened me back to reality and I snapped back to attention.

"Stop! No!" I pushed back from the man I'd once promised my life to. I wiped my lips clean with the back of my hand and my mouth brushed the jagged scar that had begun to form on my hand where my skin had been sliced open with the sharp glass.

"Macie, I'm sorry." He touched my leg. I jumped up from the couch.

"Yes," I said. "I know. Everyone is so sorry."

I turned and walked to the big picture window. The sunlight bounced in glistened rays on the water outside. I took a deep breath and turned back to Michael. He was sitting on the couch, holding his head in his hands, his elbows perched on his knees.

"Michael, I want a divorce, not a reunion. Too much has happened. Too many things..." I grabbed my belly which had begun to throb once again.

"Macie, I'm sorry," he stood up. "This isn't how I'd imagined this going. I um... I'll leave you alone."

He left. I watched him go, hoping I'd feel a twinge of regret or pain, but I felt nothing. Perhaps I'd outgrown him. He still looked good; commanding and chiseled. But how naïve could he be? Did he think he could just swoop in now and I'd shower him with forgiveness?

"Not in this lifetime," I whispered into the empty room before snuggling back down on the couch.

Sleep eluded me regardless of any drugs I'd taken at the hospital. Annaleese sat up with me and we talked into the night. She cooked a surprisingly phenomenal dinner of salmon and spinach over rice, and I couldn't help but ask where she learned to cook.

"I'm a baker by trade," she confessed as we indulged in a nightcap.

"Really?" I wasn't sure what I'd imagined she did for work, but it was something far less domestic than baking. All I knew about her, after all, was that she was Tanner's accomplice and victim. Much like me, I suppose, although I was never his accomplice. Either way, I had a hard time contemplating her helping Tanner steal millions of dollars and then going home to bake muffins and croissants.

"I work on one of the schooners in the harbor. They do three pleasure tours a day and I bake treats for each group of tourists. It's fun! It's actually how I met you guys."

"Oh?" I couldn't remember meeting her anywhere other than Michael's hotel room.

"About six years ago, you were both on my boat."

"Really? I'm sorry, I don't remember," I lied. As soon as she said it, I remembered the cruise distinctly. Michael and I were newlyweds at the time. The salty ocean air only fueled our desires for each other. We'd spent most of that tour below deck if I recall.

"Do you need any help on the boat? Are you...are you hiring?" I spit the question out before I could hold it back in.

"Do you bake?" She chuckled like she didn't believe I was serious.

"I don't, but I can learn." I took a deep breath. "Please, Annaleese, I need a fresh start. As weird as it may seem, you are the only person I know around here. I'd like it if we could become friends."

"You're serious?" She set her drink down on the coffee table and stared at me.

"I am," I laughed. It was my first real laugh in months. "Look, you and I have been through the wringer here, separately but also together. I feel like we've bonded now and I'm grateful."

"But I slept with your husband..."

"I don't blame you for that. I was supposed to be able to trust him, not you."

"I am sorry for that, Macie." She looked down at her hands as they nestled in her lap.

"No more apologies." I insisted. "Things happen for a reason. I truly believe that. Now, can I work with you or not?"

She hugged me. Our bodies interlaced together like they belonged that way.

"Friends?" she asked into my hair.

"Friends," I admitted excitedly.

For the first time, I felt myself begin to heal. As I hugged Annaleese, my breathing slowed, my heart yearning for reprieve in any form. The light at the end of the tunnel became brighter and brighter until full sunshine beamed through the cottage windows. I knew I would be okay. I wasn't alone. My journey had not been for the faint of heart, but I'd prevailed. Yes, I should probably harbor more disdain for Annaleese, but we were not so different. Our circumstances were, but we'd both made life-changing decisions in three split seconds. She'd chosen to sleep with a married man. I'd chosen to murder my stalker. Both choices led us to this couch at this moment and all I could feel was grateful. I'd felt pangs of it at the emergency room earlier as well. I was grateful for Annaleese and that wasn't something I wanted to throw away because of hatred or jealousy.

"Do you want to go out for breakfast?" she asked.

"I can't. I don't have..." I paused, stopping to reevaluate current events. "Actually yes, yes I do. I'd love to go out!"

We both smiled and retrieved our overstuffed wallets. Wallets full of Tanner's money. Wallets that were slowly leading us out of a life of tremendous despair and into one of friendship and prosperity.

"I'll drive," I grabbed my keys.

"We can walk," Annaleese suggested. "It's not far. Unless you're too sore."

"I'm great," I replied. "Let's walk."

We walked outside into the cool summer morning air, neither of us looking over our shoulders, finally.

www.ingramcontent.com/pod-product-compliance
Lightning Source LLC
LaVergne TN
LVHW041703060526
838201LV00043B/555